Island of the Dragon

Dragon Shifter Romance

Mac Flynn

All names, places, and events depicted in this book are fictional and products of the author's imagination.

No part of this publication may be reproduced, stored in a retrieval system, converted to another format, or transmitted in any form without explicit, written permission from the publisher of this work. For information regarding redistribution or to contact the author, write to the publisher at the following address.

Crescent Moon Studios, Inc.
P.O. Box 117
Riverside, WA 98849

Website: www.macflynn.com
Email: mac@macflynn.com

ISBN / EAN-13: 9781791790622

Copyright © 2018 by Mac Flynn

First Edition

CONTENTS

Chapter 1..1
Chapter 2..7
Chapter 3..13
Chapter 4..21
Chapter 5..25
Chapter 6..33
Chapter 7..39
Chapter 8..46
Chapter 9..53
Chapter 10..60
Chapter 11..66
Chapter 12..75
Chapter 13..83
Chapter 14..90
Chapter 15..97
Chapter 16..103
Chapter 17..109
Chapter 18..116
Chapter 19..122
Chapter 2..129
Chapter 21..136
Chapter 22..144

Chapter 23..150
Chapter 24..155
Chapter 25..160

Continue the Adventure..................................168
Other series by Mac Flynn.............................174

ISLAND OF THE DRAGON

CHAPTER 1

I leaned out on the railing of the elegant vessel and stared out at the calm waters of the lake in Alexandria. A cool breeze wafted by me, bringing with it the sweet smells of cooking and the sweet sound of children laughing as they raced along the shore following the path of the small ship.

I heard a flutter of sails and looked over my shoulder. Xander stood at the helm, and beside him was the captain, Magnus, and behind them was the first mate, the tall and pale Nimeni.

My dragon lord's eyes flickered between what lay ahead of us and the children that ran along the bank. He drew the ship parallel to the shore while the rough-cut sailors opened the sails to give the ship speed that matched the quick kids.

The outcropping for the temple of the lake face forced us to turn left while the children scurried onto the thin strip of land. They hurried to the end and waved to us. I strode over to the railing and waved back.

One of the young lads cupped his hands over his mouth. "Lady Miriam! Come play with us!"

I glanced over my shoulder at Xander. "Can I, Dad?" I teased.

He smiled. "I hardly believe a naughty Maiden like you deserves to play."

I climbed onto a box and from there onto the railing. The white water below me splashed against the waterline of the ship as though reaching out for me. "I'll take that as a 'yes.'"

I dove outward away from the rough waves and into the water. My water dragon drew out of my body and slipped beneath me so that I rode on its back. The children laughed and clapped their hands as I rode the beast to within a few yards of shore.

"I want a ride!"

"Me, too!"

"Please let me ride!"

I looked behind me at the dragon's long body and laughed. "I think there's enough room for all of you."

"Do you have room for one more?" a voice spoke up.

I looked past the children at a familiar figure that strode our way. I couldn't help but smile. "Were you the one who brought them here, Tillit?"

The sus stopped behind them and made a majestic bow in my direction. "I am guilty as charged, my fair Lady! I thought they might want a good swim before the water turns too cold."

I looked up and squinted at the overcast skies. "So does this world have Fall, too?"

"All the four seasons that yours does, My Lady," he assured me.

"Can we have a ride?" one of the kids pleaded.

"One last one! We promise!" another spoke up.

I patted the back of the dragon behind me. "Climb aboard. You, too, Tillit."

He picked up one of the smaller kids and waded into the water. "Much obliged for the honor, My Lady."

I grinned. "You won't think so when I'm done."

He set the kid in front of him and took a spot near the rear of my beast. "Surely you wouldn't be rough with children aboard, My Lady."

"Be rough, Miriam!"

"Yeah! We like it fast!"

I looked ahead and hunkered down. "Then hold on!"

My dragon sped forward across the surface of the water. Tillit yelped and grabbed hold of my beast as its lithe body slithered like a sonic-speed snake across the lake. We slammed through waves and skipped over rocks as we made our way along the shore. The kids cheered at every wave while Tillit winced.

The ride wasn't long. I didn't want to lose a passenger, or for Tillit to lose his lunch. Within a few minutes we slithered onto shore. "All right, everybody off."

"Aah," came the collective sound of disappointment as the children slid off the back.

Tillit lifted his leg over the dragon's back and winced as he stumbled into the water. "A very exuberant ride, My Lady. You have great control over your powers."

I shrugged as I stood on my own two feet. "It's all in the-" My dragon slipped out from beneath me and knocked its tail against my legs. I yelped as I fell backward into the two-foot deep water. My head disappeared beneath the waves and my bottom hit the soft-stone floor.

I came up coughing and with my ears ringing with the sound of the kids' laughter. Tillit himself stood over me with a twinkle in his eyes and his hand extended. "Very great control."

"Ha-ha," I retorted as I took his hand.

He helped me to my feet and I, along with the children, stumbled to the sun-drenched shore to dry off.

"You dropped something," Tillit called out.

I turned in time so see him stoop and pick up a small book that floated beneath the waters. It was the shrunken tome given to me by Crates.

I felt the color drain from my face. "Oh shit!" I ran over to him and snatched the book from his paws so I could furiously try to wipe the cover dry with my wet shirt. "Crates is going to kill me!"

"Crates of the Library?" Tillit guessed.

I nodded. "Yeah. If he found out I ruined his book-" My breath caught in my throat as I recalled that terrible griffin and its merciless justice. I scrubbed faster.

Tillit yanked the book from my hands and smiled at me. "You have nothing to worry about, My Lady."

I stared at him with wild eyes. "Nothing to worry about? He's got a griffin that eats people. That's something to-"

"The book is dry."

I blinked at him. "Come again?"

ISLAND OF THE DRAGON

He opened the tiny pages toward me and flipped through them. "See?"

I looked down and watched the dry pages flip over one another. "H-how?"

Tillit chuckled as he shut the book. "The Mallus Library hasn't survived this long without having precautions placed on all its books." He turned the book over in his hand. "I'd say with him knowing your powers he probably put a water-resistant spell on it." His eyes flickered up to me. "Though I'm wondering why you're keeping such a valuable book on you."

I breathed a deep sigh of relief and shrugged. "I asked some people in town if they could read it, but they couldn't even tell me what language it was in. Nobody seems to be able to read it, not even Apuleius."

"I can."

I arched an eyebrow at the sus. "Really?"

Tillit grinned. "Of course I can. I can't sell any books for a good price unless I know what's in them."

I nodded at the cover. "Then what's it say?"

He cleared his throat and squinted his eyes at the tiny runes on the cover. "'A History of the Dragons By Crates of Mallus.'" He started back as the book expanded to its normal size. He rubbed his scrubby beard and furrowed his brow. "I think I just said the secret password to open this thing."

I grabbed the book and tucked it under my arm before I grabbed Tillit's hand and dragged him along the shore. The children followed behind us. "Come on. You're going to the castle."

He winced. "But My Lady, think of the children if you executed me!"

"An execution!"

"Wow!"

I snorted. "You're not going to be executed, you're going to read me what's in this book so I can find out why Crates gave it to me. Now stop squirming and let's get going!"

ISLAND OF THE DRAGON

CHAPTER 2

Tillit and I met the ship at the dock where Xander grinned at me and my companion. "That is an unusual fish you have caught, but I suggest we throw him back."

I released Tillit and shook my head. "This fish is too valuable. He's going to read this-" I held up the book, "-to us."

Xander arched an eyebrow before he looked to Tillit. "You know how to read?"

The sus frowned and snorted. "After all this time and you know so little about me, My Lord? Tillit is hurt."

I shoved the book against his chest and he instinctively wrapped his arms around the cover. "Now's the time to prove your stuff. Read us a couple of pages."

Tillit opened to a few pages in and cleared his throat. "Chapter One. The beginning." He wrinkled his nose. "Crates wasn't much for exciting poetry, was he?"

I rolled my eyes. "What else does it say?"

He flipped to the beginning and browsed over a list of the unusual letters. "There's just a bunch of chapters on the supposed origins of dragons and their cousin species, like the naga." His eyes stopped roaming and he smiled. "This might be worth a look."

"What's worth a look?" I asked him.

"A compendium of legends and mysteries related to the dragons," Tillit told him as he flipped through the pages to the very back. His eyes searched the ancient words and we caught the gist of the entries through his mumbling. "The Great Bear of Bruin Bay. The Lost Legion of the Great War. The-" he paused and furrowed his brow.

"Is something the matter?" Xander wondered.

Tillit shook his head as he flipped to the very last pages. "There seems to be an entry on the Ealand of Reod Fyr."

I blinked at him. "You sounded like something got stuck in your throat."

"There is no mistake in his speech. It is the old name for the Island of Red Fire, a damned place," Xander told me. I looked up at him and my eyes widened. His face was twisted with a scowl and his eyes had a faraway look in them. "What about that place?"

Tillit browsed the pages and frowned. "It says here something about Sæ, the water, that's hidden on the island. It's supposed to be able to grant dragons enormous power, making them as powerful as the ancients of the Great War."

The color drained from Xander's face. "Where exactly is it located?"

Tillit pursed his lips and shook his head. "I don't know. It says something here about within the dragon's mouth, but I have no idea what that means. Then again-" he lifted his head and shrugged, "-that island isn't exactly my stomping ground."

ISLAND OF THE DRAGON

Xander half-turned and swept his eyes over the ship with its crew. "Then we shall have to ask someone who is familiar with the island."

He moved toward the ship, but I grabbed his arm. "Wait a sec." He glanced over his shoulder at me with that dark look on his face. "What's going on? What's this island that sounds like someone choking on hairballs?

He wrenched himself from my grasp and shook his head. "We do not have time for explanations." He marched off

I balled my hands into fists at my sides and glared at his retreating back. "Don't you-" A heavy hand settled on my shoulder. I looked behind me to find the hand belonged to Tillit.

The sus closed his eyes and shook his head. "I wouldn't follow him too close."

"But what's his problem?" I snapped.

Tillit looked past me at Xander as my dragon lord hurried up the plank. "You know him. He always gets this way when someone talks about the Red Dragons, and especially that place."

I arched an eyebrow. "What about them and that place?"

"That island is where they banished the Red Dragons that survived the War of the Lords fifty years ago," he told me. He pursed his lips and turned his attention to me. "Xander wanted all of the army to be executed, but the other dragon lords made a deal. The survivors told them where the Red Dragon's gold was in exchange for letting them live. They were all banished to the Island of Red Fire."

I frowned. "Seriously? The lords accepted blood money so they'd live?"

He grinned. "What's a dragon without his loot, and even a lord might think he doesn't have enough."

"So the Red Dragons are still there? What about the one I saw at Ui Breasail and Hadia?"

"It was a permanent banishment, so he wasn't supposed to be there," Tillit told me. He looked past me at where Xander had gone and pursed his lips. "I wouldn't have been surprised to hear that Xander killed the guy, even against King Colin's orders."

I grabbed Tillit's hand and dragged him toward the plank. "Then let's make sure he doesn't do anything that stupid with what you told him."

We followed my stomping dragon lord up the plank and to the wheel where Captain Magnus stood with the pale Nimeni at the helm. The captain shook his head. "I've been all over that island, but it beats me what the dragon's mouth is supposed to be."

"There is the Dragoi Haitzuloa," Nimeni spoke up.

All eyes turned to him and Magnus frowned. "Don't be speaking with yer strange tongue, sailor. Spit it out."

"That is what my kind calls the Cave of the Dragon," he explained.

I arched an eyebrow. "*Your* kind?"

He nodded. "Yes. I am what humans refer to as 'vampire.'"

I felt the color drain from my face. "Seriously?" I glanced at Xander. "There are vampires in this world, too?"

"Whatever tales they tell of vampires in yer old world, My Lady, Nimeni's isn't anything to be worried about. He's got himself cured of the worst of their habits," Magnus assured me.

"And what *are* those habits?" I asked him.

"That's neither here nor there, My Lady, but His Lordship was asking us about this place," Magnus reminded me.

Xander's full attention lay on Nimeni. "Where on the island is this cave?"

"Near the mountains that skirt the sea," Nimeni told him.

ISLAND OF THE DRAGON

Magnus stepped between Xander and his first mate, and stared the dragon lord in the eyes. "What are ya thinking, Yer Lordship? Ya can't be thinking of going there." Xander turned his face away and narrowed his eyes. The captain's bushy gray eyebrows crashed down. "Ya know they want yer head there, Yer Lordship. They'd kill ya as soon as they saw ya, and dump yer body into the seas without a thought."

Tillit held up the book. "We don't know if this legend is true. If that Crates thought there was something more than he would have put it in the history section."

Xander lifted his head and glared at Tillit. "But we cannot risk them finding such a power, if such a power exists."

Magnus stepped forward. "Then let me and my men go in yer stead, Yer Lordship. None would care if they saw me for Ah've not been there in such a time Ah probably wouldn't recognized meself."

Xander shook his head. "I would rather do this task myself, but I will have you take me across the Pilvien and land me at Begeondan."

I frowned and grabbed his arm. "You're not going without me. We're partners, remember?"

He turned to me and grasped my upper arms. His eyes caught mine in their unwavering gaze. "I cannot allow my partner to follow me to what may be a horrible end."

"And that's why I need to go with you, so you don't get yourself killed," I insisted.

"If something were to happen to you, I could not live with myself," he argued.

"And if something happened to you I'd lose my job as a Maiden. No dragon, no Maiden," I countered.

His eyebrows crashed down and he dropped his hands from my arms. "I will hear no more of this argument. You will remain here."

I half-turned away from him and crossed my arms over my chest. "I'm going."

"I forbid it."

"I don't care."

A chuckle interrupted our tense standoff. Everyone looked to Tillit. His large belly jiggled as he quietly made known his amusement. Xander arched an eyebrow. "What do you find so amusing?"

"That you're making a fuss when you know you're going to lose," he explained. "You should just kiss and let bygones be bygones."

Xander frowned. "I will not-"

"That's not a bad idea," I spoke up. I grabbed Xander's chin and pulled him down to my level so I could press our lips together. He was stiff for a moment before he softened to my touch. I pulled away and left him still puckered. "Well? Are we going now or later?"

Xander drew back and pursed his lips as his bright eyes studied me. He sighed and his expression softened. A crooked smile slipped onto his lips. "Now, or as soon as Captain Magnus can outfit the Blå Engel."

Magnus grinned. "She's always ready to sail, Yer Lordship. How many will we be taking on this voyage?"

"You will take only as many men as you need, and Miriam and I will be your only passengers," Xander told him.

Tillit raised one hand with his finger extended. "Don't forget Tillit, My Lord. I might not know the island, but a port is always a sus's home and I'm sure I can scrounge up some more information on this cave before you sprint into another bunch of trouble."

Magnus grinned as he looked over our group. "Then it's agreed. We sail tomorrow."

ISLAND OF THE DRAGON

CHAPTER 3

The morning dawned cold and quiet. A cool breeze swept over the deck as I wrapped my fur coat closer around me. Before me was a ship railing, and beyond that was the foggy waters of Alexandria's bay. "Why can't these adventures start out in a comfortable carriage. . ." I mumbled.

I stood on the deck of Magnus's vessel, the Blå Engel. She was a full-rigged sailing ship that stretched three hundred feet from bow to stern. The tallest mast stretched a hundred and fifty feet above my head, and between the deck and the tip were a dozen square sails of various sizes. Half of them were drawn up, and a dozen sailors worked at securing the others as a gentle breeze pushed us along the open seas.

The bay of Alexandria was far behind us, and had been for a day. All around was was stretched the blue-green waters of the ocean. I wondered if my cousin Aearion was somewhere out there and up to no good.

Tillit stepped up beside me with his satchel over his shoulder and a greenish tinge on his face. He leaned on the railing and looked out on the endless expanse of water. "It would be a carriage worth its weight in drachma if it could take us to Red Fire."

"You okay?" I asked him.

He straightened and managed a smile. "Just a little of the seas working its dark magic on my stomach. Sus weren't really meant for sea traveling, and I'll be glad when Tillit is back on land."

"How far away is it?" I asked him.

"Two hundred miles, but-" he glanced at his right toward the bow. Xander stood at the point. His back was to us. "-I think something a little closer needs your attention."

I looked past Tillit at my dragon lord and pursed my lips. "He's really not looking forward to this, is he?"

Tillit closed his eyes and shook his head. "Nope, but it's something he's needed to face for a long time."

"His mom?" I guessed.

He nodded. "His mom, and his dad. They were Joined when she was murdered."

My eyes widened. "So they were both killed?"

He looked out over the water and sighed. "Yeah. I'd never seen Xander mad until that happened, and then he was like a man possessed by demons. He was the one who led the armies of the five dragons against the Red. He killed the lord with his own hands."

I grasped the railing and bowed my head. "Ferus Draco. . ."

"Fierce Dragon, and from what I saw at that final battle he was the fiercest," Tillit told me.

I raised my head and studied the sus's pensive expression. "So you were there? When it all went down, that is."

He pushed away from the railing and turned to face me. "Yeah, I was there, but you need to be there for Xander now." A small smile slid onto his lips. "Xander doesn't need ol' Tillit to be by his side anymore, not when he's got a beautiful face like yours to look at." He jerked his head toward the brooding lord. "Go on now. He needs some cheering up."

I walked past Tillit and joined Xander at the bow. I leaned my arms on the railing beside him and studied Xander's tense face. He continued to stare ahead. I leaned forward to catch his hard eyes. "So what's out there on that island? What are we up against?"

He shook his head. "I do not know."

I pursed my lips. "Maybe that's where all the bad guys we met ran off to."

"Perhaps."

I rolled my eyes and gazed out over the endless water. "Tillit told me about the end of the war. He said you didn't want the Red Dragons to be exiled." He stiffened, but made no effort to reply. "What were they hoping the dragons would do over there?"

His eyes narrowed. "They hoped they would mend their ways."

"But you don't think that would happen?" I guessed.

"No."

"What'd you think the Red Dragons would do over there?"

Xander looked out on the waters and pursed his lips. "I hoped they would die."

I cringed. "All of them? Weren't there any kids and wives that went there?"

He pushed off from the railing and turned to face me. "All of them."

I spun around to face him and balled my hands into fists at my side. "You can't do that! They didn't do anything-"

"They murdered my mother." I froze. My face fell. He turned his face away and looked out on the sea. "They murdered my mother, and my father's death was the consequence. In one single instance, and without any warning, they destroyed my life. They took from me what I held most dear." His eyes flickered to me. "They continue to do so."

I frowned. "But that still doesn't mean you can wish death on the ones who didn't kill your parents. It's not fair to them, and it's not fair to you."

He arched an eyebrow. "Fair to me?"

I nodded. "Yeah. Holding all that hate for so long and before you know it you're just as bad as the guys who have tried to kill us. Maybe worse because you should know better."

Xander studied my face for a while before he turned away and sighed. "Perhaps you are right."

I snorted and folded my arms across my chest. "Of course I'm right. I'm your Maiden."

A hint of a smile curved the corners of his mouth upward. "No one who knows both you and I would doubt that."

"Yer Lordship! A word!" Captain Magnus called out from the platform that held the large wheel. The round wooden contraption was three feet circular and needed two men to turn it.

"Coming," Xander called back. He turned to me and gave me a genuine smile. "Thank you for the talk."

I shrugged. "Any time." He bowed his head and left me alone.

But not for long. Tillit came up beside me and studied me with a wide smile. I frowned. "What?"

"You certainly are a mare fae," he commented.

I furrowed my brow. "Why do you say that?"

He set his hand on my shoulder and met my gaze. "Because I think you could purify just about anybody, even our brooding young lord."

"Even a Red Dragon?" I teased.

ISLAND OF THE DRAGON

He dropped his hand and shrugged. "Like I said, *just about* anybody."

I glanced to my left and the seas that lay beyond the railing. "That's a lot of water."

Tillit nodded. "Yep. From coast-to-coast it's two hundred miles of open water. That's why it'll take us two days, if the winds keep with us."

"And if they don't?" I asked him.

He chuckled. "Then you'll get to see this dragon crew work their wings."

"Speaking of those, has anyone tried to fly across the sea?" I wondered.

"Once," Xander spoke up as he came up to us.

Tillit turned to him and grinned. "The bet?"

Xander nodded. "The bet."

I turned and leaned my back against the railing so I could glance from one to the other. "What bet?"

"There is a legend about a powerful dragon who made a bet with a friend that he could fly across the sea," Xander told me.

"What were they trying to win?"

He smiled as he looked down at me. "The hand of the fairest maiden on the island who they both coveted."

I snorted. "Figures. So what happened?"

"The dragon crossed the sea from the island to the continent, but he collapsed on the western shore and died soon afterward."

"That's not how I hear it," a voice spoke up. We looked over our shoulders to see Captain Magnus walk up to us.

Xander turned around and leaned his back against the railing. "How do the seas tell the tale, captain?"

"They tell that the gods rewarded the dragon's epic feat by snatching him from death and making him one of their own. A god of the air and-" he nodded at the wide expanse of water, "-this sea in particular. Some say he lives in the eye of the Eternal Storm."

I arched an eyebrow. "Eternal Storm?"

The rough captain nodded. "Aye. Ya can't miss it on this voyage."

"We should reach the safest point to view it in three hours, shouldn't we?" Xander asked him.

"Aye, and I won't go a bit closer than that. It would be only insanity that leads a man to sail into those dark clouds," the captain agreed.

I glanced at Xander. "So what were you two talking about up there?"

"Whether to dock at the harbor or go ashore in an away boat," Xander revealed.

"And?"

"We will be docking at the harbor."

I arched an eyebrow. "Isn't that more dangerous?"

"It's easier to hide a few people in the city than a ship this size along the coast," Magnus pointed out. "Better to be out in the open where we can see the trouble coming than hiding in a hole where they can throw the sail over us. Besides-" he lifted his eyes to the sails. A few of them sported a patched hole. "-it's been so long since I sailed there that I doubt I'd know my own ship among all those young braggarts with their fancy vessels."

"Captain!" Nimeni called from the platform upon which stood the wheel. Another of the sailors was at the helm.

Magnus looked out on the bow and grinned. "The seas are being kind. We're already here."

"'Here?'" I repeated.

He nodded. "There."

I followed his gaze and my eyes widened. Two hundred yards off the bow and that far off the starboard side hovered a huge cloud bank. The cloud stretched for a hundred miles and touched the true clouds in the sky. The bank was as black as soot and billowed out in thick patches that seemed to stretch out towards the ship like pudgy-fingered tendrils. Now and then a flash of lightning jumped from one cloud to the other as a warning signal to any blind captain foolish enough to venture too close to the storm.

"What *is* that?" I whispered.

"That, My Lady, is the Ikuinen Myrsky, or Eternal Storm." The captain chuckled. "Isn't she a beauty? I've sailed past her hundreds of times since I was a lad too young to even scrub the deck, and yet she still takes my breath away every time I see her."

I wrapped my arms around myself and cringed. "Yeah, um, she's something."

He turned to me and arched an eyebrow. "I'm surprised you're not agreeing with me, My Lady, you being a mare fae and all."

I shrugged. "Maybe this mare fae knows when she's not wanted, and that storm-"

"Captain!"

Captain Magnus frowned and glanced over at his second-in-command. "What is it now?"

"Aft, captain!"

Magnus looked at the rear of the ship and his eyes widened. Xander, Tillit and I followed where his eyes lay. A large sailing ship, nearly as large as the Blå Engel, sailed three hundred yards behind us.

Magnus took in a sharp breath and I heard him whisper a few words. "Gud Mín, not that one." He whipped his head to Nimeni. "Open the sails!"

"But the storm-"

"Damn the storm!" Magnus snapped as he rushed up the stairs and onto the platform with the wheel. "We can't let that ship catch us!" The sailors jumped at their orders and climbed the ropes to the rigging cross-posts.

Xander strode to the part of the deck in front of the platform and looked up at Magnus. "Captain, what is the matter?"

"Trouble, Yer Lordship! That ship is captained by a dog-faced devil that won't rest until I'm caught!"

The ship took on a burst of speed as all the sails were opened at once. I stumbled forward and Tillit caught me. I looked up into his smiling, but sickly-green face. "Where's that carriage when it's needed, eh, Miriam?"

"Captain, they are still gaining," Nimeni spoke up.

Captain Magnus looked out on the approaching ship and scowled. "It will be a dark day in helvetti before I allow that dog-faced captain to catch my ship!" He whipped his head to Nimeni and pointed at the wheel. "Take the wheel and steer us into the storm!"

My eyes widened. "You said it was insane to go into there!"

"Aye, but it's even greater insanity to let that ship catch us!" he shot back as he himself shoved his sailor out of the way and took the wheel. "Hold on!"

ISLAND OF THE DRAGON

CHAPTER 4

Captain Magnus spun the wheel and the ship turned at his command so the bow pointed directly at the storm. The seas grew rough and bounced the ship around as we approached the violent clouds.

Tillit, Xander and I stumbled around like drunken sailors as the deck tilted. Our sus friend grabbed a nearby box of crates and glared up at the captain. "If you want to die leave us-" The ship swayed to and fro. His eyes widened. He clapped a hand over his mouth and rushed to the side where he lost his second lunch. "When will I learn. . ." he groaned.

I yelped as the ship rocked violently to one side. Xander caught me in his hands and whipped his head up to glare at the captain. "There must be another way!"

Magnus cringed as the winds whipped at the sails and the boards of his ship groaned under the onslaught of the waves. "She'll make it!"

Lightning struck overhead and the electricity made the ends of my hair rise. "But will *we*?" I quipped.

"Captain, she fails to follow," Nimeni informed him.

All eyes turned back to the perusing ship. Most of her sails were tied up and her bow was turned away from the storm.

"So we can turn around, right?" I spoke up.

Magnus gripped the wheel and gritted his teeth as he tried to turn it. The behemoth of a mechanism didn't shift. He pursed his lips and shook his head. "It's too late for that."

A crack of lightning over our heads proved his point. The winds grew more violent and tore at our sails. The hope of the bright sun was obliterated by the thick black clouds that thundered its annoyance at our presence.

"Captain!" cried one of the men on the masts.

We all looked at him. He pointed at the starboard-bow where a wave as tall as the tallest mast rose from the waters a hundred feet from us. The winds threw it in our direction, and its heavy waters slammed into the ship. A great cracking alerted us to the breaking of the front mast. The seamen aboard the toppling wood leapt onto the deck and scattered in all directions as the heavy wood slammed onto the deck. Planks were cracked asunder and bits of wood flew in all directions. The sails of the ruined mast flapped uselessly atop the destruction.

A dozen sailors rushed over to inspect the damage. One of them looked over his shoulder at the captain and cupped one hand over his mouth. "Another blow like that, Captain, and she'll go under!"

Captain Magnus shook his head. "We'll need a miracle to make it out of this."

"Or a mare fae," Tillit spoke up as he turned to me with a smile. "I think now would be a good time to show off your mare skills, Miriam."

My mouth dropped open and I thrust a hand at the rough waters around us. "Are you kidding me? This is a storm, not the seas! I can't-" Another wave crashed against our starboard side. Xander pinned me between him and the mast, but he couldn't block all the cold spray that washed over me. I shuddered and looked past Xander at Tillit. "Even if it was, I don't know what to do!"

"It is our only chance." I whipped my head up and found myself staring into the unblinking eyes of my dragon lord. "You must use your powers."

I frowned. "You told me not to use it with other people watching."

"There's an exception to every rule!" Tillit assured me as the boat was thrown from side-to-side.

"But all I can do is make a stupid little dragon! How is that supposed to stop a wave even half that big?" I asked him.

Xander grasped my shoulders and met my eyes. A soft smile teased the corners of his lips. "I have faith in you, partner."

I pursed my lips. "You're really evil throwing that at me now."

"Captain!" Nimeni yelled.

The dark shadow of a large group of waves formed in the distance off the bow. The waves grew taller and the wind tore at my clothing. I could feel it in my bones, another mega wave was forming. I swallowed the lump in my throat and scooted out from Xander's protection.

The ship rocked from side-to-side as I stumbled to the bow. The mess of mast was strewn over the deck. My foot caught on the rope rigging and I fell onto my hands and knees five feet short of the tip of the ship.

A rumbling noise made me whip my head up. My eyes widened as I beheld a mammoth of a wave. It was twice as tall as the ship and four times wider. Its shadow fell over us and a shower of droplets foretold its promise of a merciless onslaught of water.

"Shit," I mumbled as I struggled to my feet.

The wave curved forward over the ship as I stumbled out of the rope and to the bow. I reached the tip just as the top of the wave licked at the middle mast at my back. My fingers began to glow blue as the water came crashing down over the ship. I threw up my hands just as the millions of gallons of water rushed down on us.

The brilliant blue light of my fae heritage sprang from my hands and spread outward and upward. The light created a huge wall in front of the ship and twenty feet beyond on either side. I winced as the water slammed into the wall. The water from the huge wave slipped over either side of the wall and crashed into the rough seas.

The weight of so many thousands of tons of water was cushioned by my wall, but the magic couldn't absorb all the pressure. A great load pressed against my hands. I felt like I was trying to stop a slow truck. My hands began to shake. My knees buckled and I fell onto one as I clenched my teeth. The light of my wall flickered as the last of the wave drained into the sea.

My wall broke. I gasped and fell face-forward. Xander's strong hands wrapped around me and I was cradled against his chest. Then I blacked out.

CHAPTER 5

My arms ached. My legs ached. My hair ached. Hell, even my gums ached. I willed my eyes open and found myself staring up at a clear evening sky. The gentle waves rocked the ship side-to-side like a cradle. I lay on the deck atop a bed of blankets. My clothes were mostly dry and smelled like sunlight.

Xander leaned into my field of vision. There was a smile on his lips. "Good evening."

"We. . .we made it out?" I whispered.

He nodded. "Yes. You allowed the captain enough time to steer the ship back to safety."

I shifted and winced. "Could you tell him not to get us *out* of safety?"

Xander chuckled as he helped me sit up. "That was a very impressive display of ability."

My face drooped. "That was insane. Don't ask me to do it again."

"But-"

"No." I pushed him away and glared at him. My head pulsed with pain. I clutched my forehead and clenched my teeth. My hand shook as tears sprang into my eyes. "I. . .I'm just a half fae. I can't perform a miracle more than once a lifetime, okay? One time you guys are going to ask me to do something and I'm not going to be able to do it, and-" I turned my face away and shook my head. "Just please don't ask me to do that kind of stuff again, okay? I'm not a hero like you guys. I'm just a girl who has a pet water dragon."

He cupped one of my cheeks in his hand and smiled at me. "You are as much a hero as any of us, my Maiden. Never doubt that."

"But she's a lot prettier to look at then some of us," Tillit quipped as he strode up to us. He adjusted his ever-present satchel and smiled down at me. "You've got a nice wall ability, My Lady. Kind of reminds of me of the purification you performed at Viridi Silva. You certainly were the hero of the day there."

I sheepishly smiled and shrugged. "That was just luck. I didn't even know what I was doing."

Tillit tapped the side of his nose and grinned. "Maybe your fae side knows more than you think."

I struggled to my feet until Xander helped me stand. My legs were wobbly, but held me up. "Maybe it should tell my human side."

The sound of heavy boots announced the arrival of Captain Magnus to our little group. He eyed me with pursed lips. "I'm sorry for putting you through that, Yer Ladyship. The seas were rougher than my old mind remembered."

I shook my head. "It's all right. I mean, we made it."

He stepped to the side and looked out over the bow. "Aye, we did."

I looked past him and caught sight of a large, rugged island of mountains and tall cliffs. A small natural harbor cut into the cliffs and created a crescent-shaped beach upon which a dozen docks of various sizes jutted out into the calm blue-green waters of the bay. Dozens of ships of various sizes, everything from a single sail to ones as large as the Blå Engel, were docked or anchored as near the sandy coast as the waters would allow.

Beyond the docks and the sandy beaches was a gentle hill up to the peak of a mountain, and on that hillside lay a ragtag city of haphazard streets and lanes. Some of the buildings were lined up beside each other only for stability, but any structure sturdy enough stood on its own at different angles than the others on the block. Rustic manor homes had adjoining lots with single-floor hovels. The crooked blocks ran up and down the hill at all angles, some going with the slope and others completely against. It was a lesson in chaos that made me shake my head.

"Where in the world are we?" I asked my friends.

"Welcome to Boldwela, Yer Ladyship," Magnus announced as he swept his hand over the scene. "A place of paradise, and Paradise is its name. Nowhere else in the world can a man-" he winked at me, "-or woman be so free as they are here."

"Or so well hidden," Xander added as he looked out on the port city with narrowed eyes.

Magnus nodded. "Aye, tis a good place to hide and a good place to search. We'll be looking for your cave after we've picked up our guide."

Xander arched an eyebrow. "A guide? Can Nimeni not lead us?"

The captain shook his head. "Nay. He just knows about the cave, he doesn't know where exactly it's sitting. Fortunately, he can find us a friend of his to lead us. For a price, that is."

"Sounds like a sus," Tillit quipped.

A crooked smile slipped onto Magnus's cracked lips. "The first rule you should know about this island is that anyone can be bought, it's just a matter of what they're wanting in return. Now then-" he turned to the deck, and I saw much of the mast wreckage was piled on the bow, "-this'll take some time to be fixing, so what say we grab some vittles ashore? I know of a good place we can go."

I arched an eyebrow. "I thought you said you hadn't been here in a while."

He nodded. "Aye, but this place has been in trade for a thousand years. It isn't likely to have gone out in thirty. Nimeni!" The pale first mate looked over his shoulder from where he stood directing the clean-up operation. "See to the ship, and if ya need me I'll be at the Ærist Phoenix if ya need me."

Nimeni bowed his head. "Aye, captain."

Captain Magnus rubbed his hands together. "All right, then, let's get you dressed and on our way."

"Dressed?" I asked him.

He grinned. "Aye. There's a trunk in me cabin you'll be wanting to look through. Otherwise yer strange dress-" he browsed my jeans and shirt, "-will catch more attention than we care to handle."

"A good idea, captain. My Maiden does stand out a bit," Xander agreed.

The captain chuckled. "You'll be wanting a change of dress yerself, Yer Lordship. Anyone walking around Boldwela in those rich a clothes is bound to get us robbed, or worse."

"And myself, captain?" Tillit spoke up as he gestured down to his worn clothes.

The captain turned up his nose. "You'll be wanting a new set just so ya don't insult the rest of us with yer stench."

Tillit raised one arm and sniffed his pit. "Smells fine to me."

Xander grasped his shoulders and turned him toward the cabin that lay beneath the wheel. "Do not argue with a man who may have you thrown overboard at any moment."

ISLAND OF THE DRAGON

I followed Xander as he pushed Tillit into the captain's cabin. The large space had a wide plank bed in the far left corner and chests along the right side. Windows at the back allowed a view of the stern and the seas we had traveled. In the far distance was a hint of dark clouds. The Eternal Storm. I wrapped my arms around myself and shivered.

"Are you well?" Xander asked me.

I dropped my arms and shrugged. "Yeah, I guess I'm just a little cold still."

"Perhaps a change of clothes would do you good," he suggested as he released Tillit and strode over to one of the trunks.

Xander opened the curved lid and stiffened. Tillit and I joined him on either side and looked into the chest. Our eyes widened as we beheld an assortment of gold treasures. There were gold plates, candelabras, goblets, and much, much more.

Tillit picked up a pair of dental teeth and arched an eyebrow. "How long has the captain been off his pirate duties?"

"Apparently not long enough to blow through his ill-gotten gains," I quipped.

"So it seems," Xander agreed as he closed the lid and moved over to the next chest. He lifted the lid and started back.

"What? Gold fingernails?" I suggested as Tillit and I hurried over.

Xander lifted a shirt out of the chest and leaned back. Tillit's eyes widened and he clapped a hand over his snout. The scent hit my less-sensitive nostrils. It was a mix of skunk and seawater with a hint of mothballs. The chest was filled with more stenched clothing.

I glanced at my horror-stricken comrades. "Please tell me these aren't the clothes Magnus was talking about."

Xander sighed and nodded. "I believe they are, but we must make the best of what we have been given."

Tillit and I cringed but together we rummaged through the chest. I pulled out a pair of woman bloomers and raised an eyebrow. Tillit glanced over and grinned. "The captain's company forgot a few things."

I shuddered and tossed it back in. "I did not need those visuals. . ."

I found a baggy pair of pants, red sash for a belt, a blouse, and a broad-brimmed pirate hat. "I've got my costume."

Tillit and Xander held a similar mess of attire in their arms. "We will dress at the stern with our backs turned away while you dress near the door," Xander suggested.

The sus grinned and wagged his eyebrows. "I promise not to look."

Xander frowned and turned the sus toward the stern. He marched him away while I hurried on with my clothes. In a few minutes I looked like a swashbuckling maid of the seas.

I looked at the back. The men were still struggling into their baggy pants. "I'm going outside," I called to them.

"We will be out in a moment," Xander replied as he hopped around with one leg in the pair of pants.

I slipped onto the deck and found the men at work scavenging what parts they could from the front mast. The captain stood nearby surveying the scene. On the starboard a few men prepared one of the away boats.

I sidled up to the captain. He looked down at me and nodded. "The look suits you, Yer Ladyship."

"If we're going to be going incognito you might want to drop the whole title thing," I pointed out.

He grinned and bowed his head to me. "A right smart, Yer-um." He furrowed his brow.

"It's Miriam," I told him.

"Aye, Miriam. A good name," he commented.

"Speaking of names-" I looked past the bow at the port. "-what's this port place called again?"

"The Ærist Phoenix. It means Rising Phoenix in the old tongue of the island," he explained.

"I know what a phoenix is in my old world, but what's it in this one?" I inquired.

He shrugged. "One of those pretty myths they tell young'uns at night so they can have pretty dreams, but I wouldn't take much stock in them being real."

"But what is it?" I persisted.

"A large bird rumored to have the ability to grant eternal life through a brush of its feathers," Tillit spoke up as he stepped out of the cabin. He wore a colorful pair of striped tan and red pants with a vest over his blouse shirt and a handkerchief over his head.

"And the rising part?" I asked him.

"It's how it gets its immortal life. The bird lights itself on fire and rising from the ashes," he told me as he joined us near the bow.

I winced. "Sounds like the bird should roll around in its own feathers."

"A child's tale. . ." Magnus grumbled

"You haven't come across one, captain?" Tillit wondered.

The captain scoffed. "Nay, and I've seen many a strange thing on the seas and islands. Not even a whisper of it being real. Now let's be off before my stomach mutinies."

Tillit glanced over his shoulder at the cabin door. "Just as soon as Xander stops wrestling with his pants-" The entrance opened and Xander stepped out.

He was attired in a pair of black tight-fitting drawers with a black coat over a white buttoned shirt. Atop his head was a black Monmouth hat like the one I wore, but with a long white feather sticking out the back. I couldn't help but admire the way the clothes hugged the perfect figure of my dragon lord.

Xander strode over to us, drew his hand off his head and gave us a sweeping bow. "How do I look?" he wondered as he straightened.

"Like a man of the sea," Magnus complimented him.

Tillit wrinkled his nose. "We certainly smell like it."

Magnus turned to the boat. "Now let's be going. The fine port and an adventure await us."

CHAPTER 6

Tillit, Xander, Magnus and I, along with a few oarsmen, climbed into the boat and were dropped into the calm water. The men rowed us to one of the longer of the many docks. The occupants, men in the ragged clothing of seamen, eyed us as we stepped onto the cracked and weathered boards. Their thick, gnarly hands deftly tied and untied the ropes that held the boats as they watched our group of four march past.

Magnus paused at a man of sixty with a sunbaked eye patch over his left eye. His face was weathered by countless winds and his black beard speckled with gray lay over his chest. He sported a dingy overcoat and worn boots.

The stranger knelt on the dock and leaned over into his small fishing boat, a single-sail vessel some thirty feet long. Magnus grinned and lifted one of his boots. A quick kick to the man's rear and he went tumbling head-first into his boat.

He rolled over and snarled at Magnus. "You damned-" His eyes widened and a grin curled onto his lips. "Well, I'll be the gods' pitcher boy. Captain Magnus-"

"A held tongue stays in the head, Captain Thatch," Magnus scolded him.

Captain Thatch chuckled as he climbed to his feet and brushed himself off. "I reckon it does, and I reckon yer the only one who calls me 'captain' anymore."

"I'd say it's because age has finally caught up to you, and an enemy did his work mighty well," Magnus commented as he settled his gaze on the man's eye patch.

Thatch brushed his fingers against the patch and sighed. "Aye, but I still mean to keep what I can before the age starts to get worse." He looked Magnus up and down. "You don't look much the worse. Been feeding long on some ransom or buried treasure?"

Magnus shook his head. "Neither. I found myself some respectable work for a stupid lord." I snorted, but quickly covered my mouth. The captain eyed me before he returned his attention to his old acquaintance. "But I've grown weary of behaving and thought I'd take up some old habits, if ya know what I mean."

Thatch smiled and nodded. "Aye, I do. Had anything in mind my old ship-" he patted the top of the railing, "-couldn't help with?"

Magnus rubbed his chin. "Perhaps, but first a drink. I'm so dry I could drink all the bay."

The old sea captain chuckled as he pointed up the hill that lay past the beach and docks. "Then off with ya. I know yer itching to have a pint or two at the Rising Phoenix."

Magnus bowed his head. "Then I'll be seeing you, Captain Thatch."

"And a hearty welcome home to you, captain," Thatch returned.

Magnus led us down the dock and onto the sandy beach. Xander sidled up to him. "An old acquaintance?"

ISLAND OF THE DRAGON

The captain nodded. "Aye, but not just that. He's the one who gave me my first command. Twas two hundred years ago if it was a day. I was hardly more than a cabin boy, but he saw something in me nobody else saw." He sighed and shook his head. "Time is cruel."

"But wisdom can only be acquired through years of experience," Xander pointed out.

A soft smile slipped onto his weathered lips. "Aye, ya speak the truth, Yer-" he paused and furrowed his brow, "-what be yer name here, anyway? I can't exactly call you by your given name being as that's not welcomed here."

Xander grinned. "I did have a great uncle of some ill-repute by the name of Nester. I shall be that name here."

"And seeing as how I'm not known here I will be Tillit," Tillit spoke up.

With the names out of the way we began the slow ascent up the gentle hill. Throngs of people joined us, some going up and others down. Men, women, and even small children hurried on their way. The foreigners were dressed in all manner of pirate attire of various deteriorating quality. Others with pale faces were covered in cloaks broad and tight. Many covered their faces in the shadows of hoods.

The locals were dressed much like the people of Alexandria, but I noticed many of the women wore the bright red sashes the mysterious Red Dragon had sported. Many of the men of Xander's age sported something else, a burnt middle finger. The blackened finger stood out against the whiteness of the rest of their skin.

I nudged my elbow into Xander's arm and nodded at a passing man with the disfigured digit. "Is that some sort of a custom here?" I whispered.

He pursed his lips and shook his head. "No. That is the mark of the war."

I arched an eyebrow. "Come again?"

"At the suggestion of Cayden's father, and at my insistence, all the males who participated in the war on the side of the Red Dragon Lord were branded by their middle finger being burned," he explained to me.

I winced. "That's pretty harsh."

He nodded. "It was, but it was necessary in order that the Red Dragons could not return without our knowing."

I furrowed my brow. "But that Red Dragon we saw only had the sash. His middle finger was just fine."

"He must have been too young to participate and can only wear the symbol of his former lord, the sash," Xander surmised.

Magnus glanced over his shoulder and frowned at us. "Could ya stop yer yapping before they start asking questions?"

"Who would ask us?" I wondered.

He nodded at a group of four sash-wearing men who stood on one of the odd-angled street corners. Their arms were folded over their broad chests, but I could see they sported the finger mark of the war. They had smirks on their faces as their red eyes swept over the area.

"Those be what passes for guards of the port," he explained to us. "One loose word and they'll be hurting you good."

I shrank down beside Xander so the burly dragon men couldn't get a good view of me. "Shouldn't we be worried about somebody recognizing Xan-Nester? Or even you, captain? They probably don't like the fact that you work for-um, Nester."

"I didn't exactly pass it around to my old mates that I was working for him," Magnus told me.

We walked past the corner with the trouble and followed a narrow, winding street up the hill. Most of the buildings were made of old planks torn from weathered ships. The doors were hatches and the shutters were porthole shutters. Even the windows were from captain's cabin quarters.

ISLAND OF THE DRAGON

Magnus stopped us at a long, squat establishment with square frosted windows that lined the single floor. The heavy wooden door looked like it more belonged to a torture chamber than a business. A small wooden sign hung over the entrance, and engraved in its weathered surface was a phoenix rising from flames.

The captain led us inside and I found it was a dingy bar. The tables were without cloth and covered in stains, some of them an ominous red color. At the back was the long stretch of bar with dirty glasses and dirtier men lined up along its top.

We took a seat at one of the rickety tables and Magnus leered at one of the buxom bar wenches who served the patrons. "Lass, some of the house's best whiskey, and two bottles of it." She sighed, but nodded and strode to the back.

Xander leaned his arms on the table and lowered his voice to a whisper. "Have we any other business here but your appetite, captain?"

Magnus chuckled. "Yer not easy to fool, Nester, but yer right. My mate's friend is to meet us here and point us in the right direction."

The bar wenched returned with her tray full of two large green bottles and four glasses. "You boys staying long?"

The old captain leaned toward her and grinned. "That would depend on what we can find."

The woman's eyes widened as he slapped her on the rear. Her eyebrows crashed down and she raised her empty tray. There was a hard smack as it came down on the old captain's hat and skull. The bar wench turned up her nose, spun on her heels, and stomped away.

Tillit poured himself some whiskey and lifted the glass to the captain. "A toast to the ladies."

Magnus pulled his hat off his head and padded it back out to its normal shape as he grumbled. "I could live the rest of my life without wenches like-" A loud slam made everyone in the establishment jump.

All eyes looked to the door and a hush fell over the crowded bar. I turned in my chair to see what was the fuss.

In the open doorway stood a beautiful young woman with long, fiery red hair. The woman looked to be about thirty with flashing dark eyes and tanned skin. She wore a black vest over a white blouse that showed her ample cleavage. Her black pants hugged her lower body and accentuated her curvaceous figure. Snug atop her hips was gun belt with a pistol on either side of her.

Captain Magnus pulled his hat over half his face and slid down in his chair so that the table hid most of him. "Shit. . ."

CHAPTER 7

The woman's dark eyes swept over the room and fell on our table. They narrowed as she beheld the slinking sea captain. "Magnus!"

Magnus's eyes flickered to Xander and his voice was a hoarse whisper. "Keep that witch away from me!" I rolled my eyes. Our captain had been reduced to a puddle of anxiety.

The woman marched across the room and stopped at our table. She put her hands on her hips and glared at Magnus. "What the hell were you thinking back there? You could've got yourself killed!"

"Um, who are you?" I spoke up.

She whipped her head around and swept her eyes up and down my person. Her lips curled back in a snarl. "Who am I? Who are you?"

I leapt to my feet and glared at her. "I asked you first."

She straightened to her full height, the same as mine, and puffed out her ample chest, which wasn't the same as mine. "I am Alice Bláur, captain of the finest sailing vessel this side of the continent and commander of the pirates who gather around this island seeking a place to spend their, well-" a sly smile slipped onto her lips, "-earnings."

I snorted. "You mean stolen treasure, don't you?"

She frowned and shoved me out of the way. "What am I doing talking to a soil brat who-" I grabbed her wrist and spun her around so she stumbled back toward the door.

"You want me to teach you what a 'soil brat' can do?" I snapped at her.

Alice rolled up her sleeves and marched up to me. Our chests bounced together as we glared at one another. "You and what fleet?"

"None of that now!" Magnus shouted as he stood. "I won't have us fighting another captain, even one from the Rache."

I furrowed my brow and glanced over my shoulder at Captain Magnus. "I thought you said the captain was dog-faced," I reminded him.

He narrowed his eyes at me. "Ah think that's enough talking for me, lass."

"Dog-faced? *Dog-faced?*" snapped the young woman. She yanked Tillit's chair out of the way and marched up to tower over the captain. She put her hands on her belted hips and leaned down so their noses nearly touched. "Is that any way to talk about your fiance?"

Xander, Tillit and my eyebrows shot up and our eyes widened. The sus gathered himself and chuckled. "Now this *is* interesting."

"It's not interesting, it's a fool's notion that I'd be marrying anyone, much less the likes of her," Magnus protested.

"The likes of *me*? You thought me fine enough before you ran off twenty years ago to the continent," Alice snapped.

Magnus slipped up beside her and clapped a hand over her mouth. "Must all you women speak too much?" he hissed.

She wrenched his hand off her mouth and glared at him. "I'll say what I please and you be damned, Captain-" Magnus leaned forward and planted a quick peck of a kiss on the end of her nose.

Alice started back. Her eyes were as wide as saucers as she touched the spot where he'd kissed her. Magnus chuckled which got her glowering again. Her eyes narrowed. "I won't be having you make a fool of me again, Captain Magnus-" Magnus, Tillit, and Xander leapt forward and all of them clapped a hand over her mouth.

Xander looked over her head at his own captain. "We must take this conversation to a more private area."

Tillit chuckled. "More like an arena. These two are feisty enough to make for quite a show."

Magnus pursed his lips. "Aye, but there be one problem. The agent we're to meet."

Alice narrowed her eyes. "Agent of who?"

"That's none of yer business, now get back to yer ship and sail off," he commanded her.

Alice drew out a pair of square handcuffs made of a green-colored metal from her corset and grabbed one of his arms. She yanked him close to her and slapped one of the pair over his wrist and placed the other on her own. "You won't be escaping this time," she growled as she gave a pull on their joined wrists.

The captain looked past her and grinned. "Suit yerself."

We all looked to the door. My breath caught in my throat as I beheld the four sash-wearing men from the corner. Their leader, a burly man a head taller than Xander, stepped forward and glared at us. The other patrons stood and scattered to the far tables in the room. The barman ducked below the bar and out of sight.

"What have we here?" the burly leader commented as he strode inside with the others at his heels. He circled our group with his Cheshire grin on his lips. His attention especially lay on Alice and me. "A couple of pirates not playing nice? You know the rules of the island."

Alice glared at him. "Learn them yourself. So long as we're not brawling you can't lay a finger on-"

"Shut your mouth," the dragon snapped as he stopped beside Xander. He studied my dragon lord and pursed his lips. "Don't I know you?"

Xander grinned. "Perhaps I robbed a ship you were on."

The leader leaned close to Xander's face and shook his head. "Not there. Somewhere with fire. Somewhere like-"

"Yer wasting our time," Magnus spoke up. The dragon whipped his head to him and narrowed his eyes. Magnus straightened and glared back at him. "If yer done pestering us than we'll be off." He gave a tug on the handcuffs and smiled at Alice. "Looks like yer coming, too, my-" The dragon ruffian clapped a hand on Magnus's shoulder.

"I will tell you when you can leave," he growled.

Magnus sighed and glanced at Xander. "Ya won't be minding, will ya, Nester?"

Xander smiled and shrugged. "We have no choice."

Our captain whisked Alice off her feet and spun them both around. Her feet slammed into the side of the dragon leader's face. He turned a full circle before he collapsed in a heap on the floor.

ISLAND OF THE DRAGON

The other three dragons cried out and lunged at us. Xander slipped beneath one and lifted him up by his chest before he tossed him across the room and onto a table. The table broke beneath his weight and both fell to the floor unmoving.

Tillit drew off his satchel and whacked another in the gut. The dragon doubled over and his eyes bugged out. Tillit slammed his bag on the dragon's head and our foe dropped to the floor. He twitched a little, but didn't try to get up.

I nodded at Tillit's bag as he slipped it back over his shoulder. "What do you have in that thing?"

He grinned. "A few gold bars to trade."

That left one more foe. He looked at his fallen friends, and turned tail and ran for the door. "No ya don't!" Magnus growled. He rushed the person with Alice still in his arms.

"Let me go!" she growled as she squirmed in his hold.

Her thrashing made Magnus trip over a chair and together the pair crashed into the wall close to the door. Magnus landed on his rear and Alice dropped onto his lap and stomach, forcing the wind out of him. The dragon rushed out of the entrance and down the street out of sight.

Magnus growled and pushed her off, but he ended up yanking his own hand with her. "Now look what you've done!" he snapped.

Alice leapt to her feet and yanked on his chain. "What *I* did? What the hell are you thinking tussling with the weard?"

"The what?" I spoke up.

She whipped her head to me and narrowed her eyes. "This is none of yer business, girl."

My eyebrows crashed down and I marched toward her, but Xander grabbed my arm. "We do not have time to squabble."

Tillit stepped forward and nodded. "Yeah. That one weard is sure to bring friends."

Xander grasped my hand and pulled me toward the door. "We must return to the ship and find another way to contact the agent." Tillit followed us.

Magnus gave a hard tug on the handcuffs and glared at Alice. "Get these off."

Her face flushed. "I-I can't." That made us all freeze and turn to the pair.

His eyes widened. "Whadda ya mean ya can't?"

She turned her face away and stuck her lower lip out. "I don't have the key with me."

Magnus threw up his arms and took one of hers with him. "Just like a woman!"

"Hey!" Alice and I shouted together.

"She will have to come with us, at least for the present," Xander suggested.

Alice frowned and tugged on the chain. "I'm going nowhere with you. I have a client to meet here, and-" Shouting from the street caught our attention.

Tillit peeked out the door and yanked his head back in before he turned to us. "We have company."

His pronouncement was followed by the man's shout. "That one! The Rising Phoenix!"

"This way!" Alice snapped as she spun around and pulled Magnus to the bar.

The captain grabbed the chain and dug in his heels. "What a minute! Where are ya taking us?"

She whipped her head around and glared at him. "Does it matter?" There was more shouting from outside, this time louder and with more voices.

Tillit raised his hand. "I vote we follow her."

"Seconded," I spoke up.

She gave a hard tug on the chain. "Then come on."

We followed her behind the bar where the bartender still hid with his bottles. She kicked him in the side. "Come on, Ashleigh, open it up." He brushed a bottle out of the way and revealed a lever which he pulled. The floor at the far side of the bar dropped down and became a short ramp to an underground tunnel. She grinned and nodded her head to him. "Thanks, and don't forget to close it this time."

Alice led us down the short ramp and into a tunnel carved from the dirt and stone. Tillit was the last to step off and his foot nearly caught on the ramp as it swung up. With its closing we were engulfed in darkness.

CHAPTER 8

I clung to Xander's arm and swept my eyes over the complete darkness. "Um, was this really a-"

"Ssh!" Alice snapped.

A noise of heavy boots was heard above us as a dozen men entered the Rising Phoenix. A couple of pairs of feet clomped across the floor boards to the bar where they paused.

"Bartender." The voice was smooth, calm, and familiar. My eyes widened and my heart skipped a beat as I recognized the silky voice of the Red Dragon we'd met on previous occasions.

There was a faint squeak as the bartender exited from his hiding place. "Y-yes, sir?"

"I was informed that those who attacked the weard were a group of five people, and one of them was a human woman," the Red Dragon mused. I swallowed hard.

"I'm not really sure-"

ISLAND OF THE DRAGON

"Of course you are," the Red Dragon interrupted. "Anyone fit to be the keeper of the Rising Phoenix's legendary stock is more than fit to know who comes and goes through its door." His boots clomped around the bar and stopped a few feet short of the secret entrance. He lowered his voice to a soft whisper. "The Lord Red Dragon would appreciate your assistance in finding these five strangers." I felt Xander stiffen.

There was a brief pause before the Red Dragon chuckled. "I see. You are incapable of betraying your patrons because you are incapable of speaking." The red Dragon took one step and shifted one foot. "Remove him from my sight, and search the premises."

Someone stepped forward. "But sir, the Rising-"

"I am well aware of the fondness held for this establishment, but those who attacked our men must be found," he insisted.

"Very good, sir." The bartender was led away and we heard the footsteps stomp all over the floor in their efforts to find us.

"Follow me," I heard Alice whisper.

I felt Tillit walk past us, but Xander didn't move. I gave a soft tug on his arm. "We have to go."

"The Lord Red Dragon. . ." Xander whispered.

I gave him a hard shake. "We have to leave, so snap out of it!" I hissed.

I felt him shake himself. "Yes, you are correct."

He took my hand and led me through the abyss. We pounded the hard ground as the tunnel led us in a meandering direction across the hillside.

"Where. . .exactly. . .does. . .this go?" Tillit puffed. He gagged and clapped his hand over his large nostrils. "Don't tell me-"

"Stop yer whining or get yer sorry arse back to the pub!" Alice snapped at him.

"What. . .choices. . ." Tillit gasped.

I frowned. "Where are we-" A weak glow appeared at the end of the tunnel.

We stopped beneath the soft light which appeared from the ceiling. An old wooden ladder led up to the hole which was a round wooden hatch. Alice climbed the ladder, but she only made it a few rungs before one arm was dragged down by the weight of a certain sea captain.

She glared down at him and tugged on the chain. "The weard haven't run this island for fifty years because they're a little smarter than the stupid populace. They're a lot smarter, and they're going to find that hatch sooner rather than later, so-" she took a step onto the next rung and yanked on their joined chain, "-get those old joints moving."

"Damn wench. . ." Magnus grumbled as he climbed the ladder close behind her. He looked up and his frown turned to a lecherous grin as he admired her assets. "Ya haven't changed much."

Alice's eyebrows crashed down and she kicked him in the face. "Enough of that, ya worthless old hull scum!"

He shook off the hit and chuckled. "As fiery as ever."

Alice growled and returned her attention to the ladder which she climbed. Tillit followed the pair. I turned to Xander. He looked back in the direction we'd come. His face was furrowed and his lips were pursed.

I set a hand on his shoulder. "You okay?"

He didn't look at me as he replied. "There cannot be another Lord Red Dragon. I killed him myself."

"Maybe they elected a new one like they need to do at the Heavy Mountains," I suggested.

Xander shook his head. "The Red Dragons were loyal to their lord, and no one else.

"Maybe he had a kid?" I persisted.

"His Maiden was barren."

I started back. "She. . .you mean she couldn't give him an heir?"

He studied the darkness a while longer before he turned his focus on the ladder. "That is for another moment. Now let us climb."

I frowned, but climbed the ladder with Xander behind me. Our companions had removed the cover and Tillit peered down the hole at us. He helped me over the lip and onto a wood floor. I took a deep breath from the exertion and immediately regretted it.

The air stank like a humid outhouse. Steam floated above our heads like an eternal fog. Large shallow pools of wood strips strapped together with metal rings stood in neat little rows and columns. Women marched in place to a silent music as they chatted away to one another, their bodies knee-deep in soapy water filled with clothing.

I clapped a hand over my nose as I climbed to my feet. "Where are we?"

"The local laundry and dying factory," Tillit told me. "That pleasant smell is the urine used to clean the cloth."

"This way," Alice barked.

She guided us through the thick steam and to the rear of the factory. A back door led out onto an empty narrow street. Xander shut the door behind us and we pressed against the stone wall of the large building.

"What now?" I asked my smelly companions.

Alice raised her imprisoned arm. "We have to get to my ship so I can fix this."

"We'll get back to me own ship to do that job," Magnus insisted.

She glared at him. "Has your bad eye gone blind? These are magic handcuffs created by the naga. They can't be broken except with a naga tail."

"You have a naga with you?" I asked her.

She wrinkled her nose. "Of course not. I just have the tail, and we're going for that now."

"I'd hate to get into the middle of this cheery argument, but there was a point to us coming ashore," Tillit reminded our group.

I winced. "The guide Nimeni set us up with."

Xander swept his eyes around the area. "If the guide ever reached the tavern they are sure to have been frightened off by the weard."

Alice arched an eyebrow. "Where *exactly* was this guide supposed to take you?"

Magnus yanked on the chain. "That's none of yer business, woman."

She yanked back on the chain. "It is if we're stuck together."

"That's yer fault for clapping these damned things on us."

"If you hadn't left me at the altar I wouldn't need to keep you by my side!"

"*Yer* the one who left me!" Magnus snapped.

Alice narrowed her eyes. "Ya lying little soil lover. When I get free I'm going to claw yer eye out and use yer fake one as a marble."

"That is enough," Xander spoke up as he set a hand on Magnus's shoulder. "We do not have the luxury of argument if we hope to make it back to any of our ships."

Tillit glanced up and frowned. "I think we should be trying to find that Dragon Cave."

"Why?" I asked as I followed his gaze.

My blood froze as I glimpsed large shadows pass over our heads. They were a dozen dragon men clothed in the red sashes and bearing the tell-tale black finger. They swooped over us and in the direction of the harbor.

Xander rushed around the corner of building and the rest of us followed him. He led us to the front where the hillside allowed us a clear view of the harbor. The dozen dragons were joined by four dozen more of their comrades.

ISLAND OF THE DRAGON

The flock swooped over the roofs and across the beach to the bay waters toward the ships.

Magnus's eyes widened. "My ship!"

Cannon shots were fired from the Blå Engel as the dragons flew around its repaired masts. The dragons easily evaded the thick black balls, but not the earth-rattling explosions that followed. The bursting of the balls sent shock waves through the air and shook the buildings and trees.

The balls exploded into thousands of tiny metal bits that clung to the dragons like spitballs. The dragons grabbed the bits and tried to pull them off, but at a yank small spikes sprang from the metal and stuck into their fingers and hands. Some of the spikes shot out and slammed into the unexploded parts, setting them off in a terrible chain reaction of pain. The dragon men dropped from the sky like heavy rocks and splashed around the Blå Engel. The ship opened her sails and sailed out of the bay.

I looked to Magnus and jerked a thumb at the battle. "What the hell were those?"

The captain grinned. "Trap balls filled with spikes and Dragon's Bane. Nimeni loads them himself."

"Now it seems we must find our guide," Xander mused.

Alice arched an eyebrow. "Where was this guide going to take ya?"

Magnus frowned and yanked on the chain. "If we're stuck together than ya may as well know. We need to be heading for the Cave of the Dragon."

Her eyes widened. "Dragoi Haitzuloa?"

"You know if it?" Xander asked her.

She snorted. "Aye. The vampires who raised me told me tales of it when I was a lass."

I raised an eyebrow. "You were raised by vampires?"

She glared at me. "Aye. What do ya think raised me?"

51

I shrugged. "Harpies?"

Xander stepped between us as Alice glared daggers at me. He turned to the said harpy. "Was your arrival at the Rising Phoenix because you were hired to lead a group to the Cave?"

Alice nodded. "Aye, and-" her narrowed eyes flickered to Magnus, "-now I see I didn't ask enough for the job."

Magnus glared straight ahead of him and balled his free hand into a fist. "Damn that Nimeni. I'll have his hide for this. . ."

"Can you lead us to the cave?" Xander requested.

Captain Bláur folded her arms across her chest and pulled Magnus against her side. She snarled at him and shoved him away. "Aye, but the price just went up."

Xander nodded. "Whatever it takes."

CHAPTER 9

"What it'll take is a boat," Alice told him.

Magnus yanked on the chain. "We're not going on yer ship."

Alice returned his yank with one of her own and glared at him. "My ship won't fit where we need to go. We need a smaller one."

"There's the old sea dog Magnus met on the docks," Tillit suggested.

Magnus pulled on Alice's chain and nodded. "Aye, Captain Thatch will take us where we need to go."

Alice frowned and yanked on the handcuffs. "Captain Thatch? I wouldn't trust that bilge rat with a rotten fur."

He drew her to him and stuck his nose against hers. "Ya got a better idea?"

She pursed her lips, but turned her face away. "Fine. Let's get this finished so I can cut this fool off me."

"Agreed," Magnus replied.

"Um, one problem," I spoke up as I studied the distance between where we stood and the dock. "How do we get there without being noticed?"

Tillit turned around to face the laundry factory and rubbed his bristled chin with one hand. "I might have an idea."

In a short while, and after a little bartering on Tillit's part, we found ourselves the proud owners, and wearers, of five black sheets. As we wrapped ourselves in them I glanced at Xander. "Is this seriously going to-" A pair of black-cloaked pale people walked past us. "Never mind."

"This is what many of the vampires wear to protect their sensitive skin from the sun," Alice explained.

I furrowed my brow. "Nimeni doesn't wear a cloak.

Magnus tried to pull the cloth over his head and ended up wrapping it tightly around the back of his neck. "He uses a lotion. . ." he grumbled as he fought with the sheet.

Alice rolled her eyes as she grabbed the front edge of the sheet and drew it over his head. "You really are impossible."

"Let us hurry," Xander commanded our strange little group.

We moved as a pack, Alice and Magnus having little choice in the matter, down the winding streets toward the beach.

"Get down!" Xander hissed.

We hit the wall of a nearby house as another flock of dragons flew over our heads. They swooped down low over the bay waters and picked up their downed companions before they turned back and flapped up the hill to the top. I followed their route and watched them fly over the top of the hill and disappear on the other side.

"Where are they going?" I whispered.

"To the Keep," Alice told me. "It's what the weard call their barracks."

"Sounds comfy," I quipped.

"As comfortable as a bed of iron spikes," she returned.

Xander slipped off the wall and down the hill. We followed, and I sidled up beside him. I could see part of his face. It was tense. "You okay?"

"I am fine."

"What you are is really quiet," I pointed out.

His eyes flickered over the many dragons who wore the red sash and the black mark. "I had hoped to never see the Red Dragons again, and now I find myself among them to stop them from gaining a great power."

I slipped my arm beneath his sheet and clasped his hand. "*We're* trying to stop them."

He pursed his lips. "I hope we can."

We reached the beach and strode across the dock to where Captain Thatch stood in his boat tending to some nets. He looked up at our coming and let out a great laugh. "Have you found religion, captain?"

"We found suitable cover, and need a boat to take us somewhere," Captain Magnus replied.

Thatch arched an eyebrow and walked to the side of his boat closest to the dock. "Take you where?"

"To the Stáncarras of Whyte," Alice told him.

He started back and his eyes widened. "Are you mad? No one can get through those."

She grinned. "I can, but only if you follow my directions perfectly."

Thatch eyed the young woman and grinned. "I'll gladly follow ya to my cabin," he offered as he gestured to the small tent-like structure at the rear of the boat.

Alice narrowed her eyes and threw a punch at the captain. Unfortunately, she threw a punch with her chained hand. Magnus was yanked forward and crashed into his fellow captain. The two toppled over into the boat, sending

Alice with them. She landed atop them in a heap of squirming arms and thrashing legs.

"You fools!" she snapped.

"Who's the fool who got us into this mess?" Magnus growled. Alice swung her fist at him, the free one this time, but he caught it in his palm. "Are ya to be our guide or our tormentor?"

"Both," she growled.

Tillit glanced at Xander and I as we stood on the dock. "This could be a long boat ride."

Captain Thatch looked up at us and grinned. "Not if-" he winced as the pair above him scuffled, "-not if we can get on our way. You won't find a boat on these piers faster than mine."

Xander glanced over his shoulder back at the city and frowned. "It appears we have no choice."

Everyone followed his gaze. My pulse quickened as I beheld four dozen dragon swoop over the top of the hill. They split into groups of four, each taking a portion of the city. Two of the groups flew downward toward the beach. All their comrades were picked up which meant only one thing: they were headed right for the docks, and us.

"Inside!" Xander shouted.

We all leapt into the boat just as the swooping dragons reached the beach. They drew out their swords and drew their arms back as they aimed straight for us.

Thatch crawled out from beneath the squirming pile of distempered pirate captains and ran to the only mast. He yanked on a single rope which bound the two square sails closed. They dropped open and the wind filled their cloth forms to push the boat forward.

The old captain hurried to the helm of his ship, a small wheel at the rear, and grabbed the steering contraption. He spun the wheel and the bow of the ship turned away from the docks.

ISLAND OF THE DRAGON

But not very far. We were all thrown forward as something abruptly stopped the ship from sailing farther away.

"The blasted rope!" Thatch shouted at us as he pointed at the bow. The boat was tied to the dock.

Xander and Magnus, dragging his unwilling companion, leapt to the bow. One end was attached to the boat and the other to the dock. Magnus drew out his sword and sliced the four-inch rope clear through.

"Not that way!" Thatch snapped as he frantically spun the wheel. "What dog taught you that!"

Magnus turned to him with his cutlass in hand and grinned. "You did."

"Stop looking back and start looking up!" Tillit yelled at us.

The shadows of the weard flew over us. Two of the four landed in the middle of the boat, rocking the small vessel from side-to-side. Tillit and I with our 'soil brat' legs fell onto the deck, but the others locked their legs and kept their stance as our foes pointed their swords at us.

Alice drew her sword and lunged at one of the dragons. Magnus took the other. Their close connection forced them to battle between the pair back-to-back to one another.

Alice glanced over her shoulder and grinned. "Just like old times, isn't it, Magnus?"

He returned her grin with a sly smile of his own. "Ya still remember the Battle of Taubenloch?"

She laughed. "Not a bad idea."

The pair ducked at the same time. The sudden loss of their opponents meant the dragons stumbled forward. Magnus and Alice pointed their swords upward and the dragons fell onto their blades. The pair of pirates lifted their foes up with their swords and threw them overboard.

The boat turned toward the opening of the bay and cut through the waters as the other two dragons pursued us.

Tillit raised himself onto his knees and dropped his satchel in front of him. He rummaged around before he drew out a thin tube of metal a foot long and two inches in diameter. There were six cords on the bottom.

I looked from the tube to Tillit. "What's that?"

He grinned. "Deus ex machina."

Tillit stood and pointed the top at the dark shadows in the sky. He grabbed one of the cords and gave a yank. Out from the tube shot a stream of colorful confetti. The flapping bits of squares flew up into the sky and did a barrel roll to follow the tail of one of the dragons. I had to blink twice as the stream dipped and turned with our foe.

The other dragon swooped in low. Tillit spun around and pointed the small tube at him. He pulled another cord and shot off another round of living confetti. The range was close enough I could see tiny wings on the bits of paper.

Alice's eyes widened and she whipped her head to Tillit. "What god told ya to hold vampiri de hârtie in that satchel?"

Tillit shrugged. "The evil kind."

"Vampire *what*?" I yelped.

"Paper vampires, but don't worry. I've trained them to only attack winged dragons," he assured us.

I grabbed the front of his coat and glared at him. "But what's going to happen when they don't have any more winged vampires to attack?"

He sheepishly grinned. "Well, my plan was always that I wouldn't be around when that happened."

The battle raged above us. The dragons swooped and ducked to avoid the cutting corners of the paper vampires, but always keeping with our boat. One of the dragons flipped over and swiped his sword across the body of the swarm. A dozen pieces of bat fluttered onto the water, but the others were not even slowed. They latched onto him and I glimpsed little teeth grow out of their paper fronts.

ISLAND OF THE DRAGON

The dragon screamed as their teeth latched onto him. He dropped his sword and pawed at them, but they stuck like leeches. The dragon lost control and crashed down into the water. He disappeared beneath the surface and didn't come up.

That left one more. The final dragon dove down and flew beneath our lowest sail. Xander jumped him and together the pair went rolling along the deck. My dragon lord ended up on the bottom with the black-fingered dragon above him.

Our foe's lips curled back in a sneer as he raised his sword to bring the point down on Xander's chest. "Say hello to your father, Ferus Draco."

The paper vampires slammed into the back of the winged dragon. His eyes widened and he leapt to his feet as he tried to dislodge the paper from his back. The little vampires sank their fangs through his shirt and into his flesh. The dragon screamed and stumbled around the deck.

Tillit stuck out his foot. The dragon tripped and flipped overboard, taking the vampires with him. They splashed into the water. I rushed to the side and looked out at the water. Only a few bits of wet paper floated on the surface until they, too, sank beneath the waves.

We sailed past the mouth of the bay and into the safety of the open seas.

CHAPTER 10

I heard a stomping behind me and turned around to find Alice marching up to Tillit with Magnus dragged behind her. She grabbed the sus by the throat and yanked him into her face. "Don't ya ever do something that stupid again."

Tillit shrugged. "It worked, didn't it?"

"They could've drained us dry!" she snapped.

Magnus laid a hand atop hers and looked her in the eyes. "That's enough, Captain Bláur. We need ya to lead us through the rocks, not strangle the best nose we've got." She snarled at Tillit one last time before she pushed him away.

Tillit still held the rocket tube, and when she shoved him backward he stumbled over some of the piles of rope that littered the area around the mast. His back hit the mast and he dropped the tube. The contraption hit the floor butt-first and one of the ropes snagged beneath its own weight, pulling it out slightly.

ISLAND OF THE DRAGON

A plume of confetti shot out of the tube and high into the air above the mast. The little square bits of paper flitted around as a flock until they paused just beyond the bow. I could feel their non-existent eyes settle on the fresh blood on the deck. *Our* fresh blood.

Magnus whipped his head to Alice and glared at her. "Now ya've done it!"

She pointed an accusing finger at Tillit. "He's the fool who has that stupid thing!"

The paper vampires inserted their opinion into the conversation when they dove down, giving the sails a wide berth as they ducked beneath the lowest one. We all hit the deck as they swooped low for our exposed faces. They missed my nose by a nose and flew across the deck toward the wheel. Thatch dove down, releasing the wheel from his control. The winds of the open sea pushed against the sails and pulled the wheel, turning the ship a hard right toward the island and the steep, rocky cliffs.

Thatch scrambled to his feet and grabbed the spinning wheel. He grunted and turned the boat away from certain doom. "Get those damn things out of my way!"

Magnus whipped his head to our pilot. "Can't this old tub go any faster?"

Thatch held the wheel steady and glared at him. "If you've got a sail up yer arse I'm willing to use it!"

My eyes widened and I released Tillit to look down at my heavy coat. "Our clothes!" Everyone glanced at me as I lifted my eyes to them. "We have to strip!"

Tillit arched an eyebrow. "Come again?"

"Those things are paper, aren't they?" I asked him. He nodded. I pointed at the sails. "And they didn't go through the sail to get at us which means they *can't.*"

Xander smiled and drew off his pirate coat and hat. "You never cease to amaze me."

"Compliments later, stripping now," I ordered him.

Alice's eyes flickered to Magnus and she cringed. "Can we exempt this old dog?"

"Stop yer yapping, she-hound, and get yer coat off!" Magnus barked as he stripped off his own attire, tearing his coat sleeve to get it off his handcuffed hand.

As we removed our attire the fluttering death confetti circled around and dive-bombed us again. Xander, Tillit and I opened our coats and held them in front of ourselves. Most of the vampires flew around us, but some collided with our coats. Their tiny paper wings caught in the rough cloth and they flapped helplessly. We rolled up our coats and trapped them inside.

The remaining paper vampires charged our two captain friends. Alice held her blouse in her hands and Magnus his coat. The blood-sucking pests turned, but the pair lunged forward and wrapped their clothing around the vampires, trapping them in the stench of their worn clothes.

Magnus held up his coat, but all his attention was on Alice. Her short coat lay across her shoulders, one of its sleeves torn open. She had used her blouse to capture the beasts, and without her billowing shirt there was only a primitive mess of wide white bandages wrapped around her ample assets.

She glared back at him and held up her blouse. The thin cloth allowed us to see the shadows of the squirming vampires. "Keep looking and I'll make sure ya wear these," she growled.

Magnus averted his eyes as I held up my own squirming coat. "So what do we do with these things now?"

Xander turned to Tillit. "Can you return them to the tube?"

Tillit studied his own squirming clothing and wrinkled his nose. "Yeah, but not on a shaky boat like this."

"She's the steadiest boat there is on these waters!" Thatch shouted from the wheel.

"It's a delicate operation stuffing them into the tube. It can't be done just anywhere," Tillit rephrased.

Magnus tilted his head back and looked up at the sails. "I'll be guessing these creatures can go a long while without rest, aye?"

"Aye aye, captain," Tillit confirmed.

"Then why don't we strap them to the sail posts and I'll stand at the bow with my wings. That'll lure them to me and get us on faster," he suggested.

Xander smiled as he took Tillit and my cloth. "A brilliant idea, captain."

Soon our six 'bags' were strung up on the lowest cross post. Magnus and Alice strode to the bow and the old sea captain turned to face the mast. His wings burst from his back and spread over the sides of the boat and out into the water. My hand flew to my mouth as I beheld the countless scars, cuts, and tears in the old leather and bones. The condition of his wings didn't stop the bags of paper vampires from pushing against the front of the clothes. They pulled the post with them thereby pulling the entirety of the ship and increasing our speed.

Magnus noticed my gawking and grinned. "Impressive, aye?"

"More like foolish," Alice quipped.

I pointed a finger at his wings. "Do they. . .do they still work?"

"It's been a while, but let's see." He flexed the wings and gave a single flap. A cool wind blew over us. The captain grinned. "A little worn, but as good as when I was a lad."

Thatch shook his head. "Age is a terrible thing. As cruel and unforgiving as the seas."

I moved to Tillit's side and leaned toward him. "Speaking of cruel seas, where are we going again?"

"The Rocks of Whyte, so named because a human by that name was the first to mention it," he told me.

"And they're scary because-?"

"Because no one's ever sailed that water and not been dashed upon the rocks," Magnus spoke up.

Alice yanked on their chain and glared at him. "Of course they've been navigated. The vampires mapped them out ages ago."

"There's no map in the world that's charted them," Magnus argued.

"There is."

"There isn't."

"There is."

I rolled my eyes. "Are you two sure you didn't get married because you sound like an old married couple to me." The pair whipped their faces to me and growled. I held up my hands and took a step back. "Easy there. We're on the same side."

"How far until we reach the Stáncarras of Whyte?" Xander spoke up.

Alice gave me one last glare before she turned to Xander. "A half hour, but only ten minutes will decide whether we're to live or die this day."

"Plenty of time to regret what we're doing," Tillit quipped.

Alice's eyes flickered from the sus back to my dragon lord. "What exactly *are* we doing in those caves?"

"What stories do the vampires tell of them?" Xander asked her.

She folded her arms and shrugged. "Just the usual stories about old caves. There's always been said to be some sort of connection to dragons, hence the name, but other than that there's nothing much to say."

"So what kind of a treasure are we looking for," Thatch spoke up.

Xander and I turned to Tillit. "What details does the book contain?"

ISLAND OF THE DRAGON

Tillit drew out the Crates Library book and flipped to the back of the book. "It says here that the dragons of old buried their most precious treasure in the deepest part of the caves."

"That water that gives dragons the power of the old dragons?" I guessed.

He traced his finger along the pages and furrowed his brow. "It's kind of hard to read what's been written. I think that librarian needed an editor to look at this before he decided to bind it."

Alice arched an eyebrow. "Water that gives dragons some ancient power? Is that what you're after?"

"That is what the Red Dragons may be find if we do not stop them," Xander told her.

She snorted. "If they haven't found it in fifty years why would they find it now?"

Xander turned toward the island and swept his eyes over the rocky cliffs. "If these rocks are so treacherous as you say then the secret would be well-kept. Regardless, we shall soon find out for ourselves."

CHAPTER 11

The paper vampires sped us along, and the thirty minutes turned into ten. The rugged coast of the island dipped inward, but the rocks spread a further hundred yards out into the water. Many of the stones towered over the small boat as Thatch piloted us into the watery field. Magnus drew his wings back into his body. The bats calmed and the boat slowed.

Unfortunately, the waters didn't calm. The seas crashed against the rocks and stirred itself into a frothing frenzy. Our boat rocked from side-to-side so violently that I was forced to grab the mast.

Tillit joined me and wrapped his arms around the post. His face looked a little green as he hugged the wood. "Isn't this fun. . ." he muttered.

"Not a problem!" Thatch shouted as he let out a laughed and spun the wheel. The boat turned sharply to avoid one of the giant boulders. The rough stone skimmed the planks and chipped some of the wood. "Now where's that cave?"

Magnus and Alice stumbled into the side of the boat and grabbed the edge. Alice whipped her head around and glared at our driver. "It's not the rocks ya should be watching out for, you fool!"

"Good, because we're almost out!" Thatch replied as he pointed out over the bow.

The field of rocks had one open spot, a circular area near the cliffs. The sea spray hit me in the face, but I shook it off and squinted into the distance. I pointed at the cliffs. "What's that?"

Everyone followed where I pointed. It was a shadowed hole at the bottom of the towering wall of rocks.

Alice stepped up to the side of the ship and set her hand on the railing as she looked out on the churning waters. "That's the cave, but keep your eyes open."

"For underwater rocks?" Xander asked her.

She shook her head. "It isn't the rocks we have to watch out for. It's Sălbatic."

I blinked at her. "The what?"

"It means 'Wild' in the language of the vampires, and it's the creature that guards the entrance to Dragoi Haitzuloa," she explained.

"So it looks like what?" I persisted.

She pursed her lips. "You'll know it if it comes, and let's hope it-" Something big and heavy slammed into the bottom of the boat, pushing the bow out of the water and shoving us to the side.

Xander fell against me and reached around either side of me to grab the mast himself. He looked over his shoulder at Thatch. "Did we hit a rock?"

Thatch shook his head as he steered the boat away from the spot. "No rock ever shoved me around."

"It's Sălbatic! He's found us!" Alice shouted.

I frowned. "What is a-" My question was answered when a huge column of water exploded just off our starboard side.

I threw up one arm as we were sprayed with thick, heavy drops of water. The rainfall was loud, but not as loud as the screeching cry that echoed off the rocks. I lowered my arm and gasped.

Beside the boat, hovering twenty feet in the air, was a handsome young man. His upper body was that of a human with powerful muscles. He was clean-shaven which gave him the appearance of a man of twenty. At his sides hung his muscled arms which ended in long fingers with four-inch long nails.

His long silvery hair reached past his waist and floated around him like a funeral shroud. Everything below the waist, however, was like that of a naga with gray-and-dark blue scales that climbed down a snake-like body that disappeared into the dark depths of the water. The only difference lay on the creature's back. A single row of sharp spines stretched from his waist and down his snake body.

"What the hell is that?" I yelped.

"Sălbatic!" Alice yelled.

"Yeah, but what the hell *is* he?" I persisted.

"A demon that'll steal our souls if we don't get out of here!" she snapped as she whipped her head to Thatch. "Head to the port side and skirt the rocks!" Thatch nodded and turned the wheel, but not fast enough.

The creature slithered up beside us and lowered himself so he stood equal to the deck. His bright blue eyes swept over our small crew and stopped on me. I felt a cold chill slip into my body as a sly smile slipped onto his pale lips. He stretched out his hand toward me.

I shocked myself when I let go of the mast and walked toward him. I tried to tell my body to turn away, but it wouldn't listen. All it knew was those beautiful eyes were calling to me, and I had to obey.

"Grab her!" Alice shouted.

Xander wrapped his arms around me. A flash of red-hot anger swept through me. I thrashed in his hold and snapped my teeth at his hands.

Sălbatic glared at my dragon lord and raised his hand. A narrow column of water sprang from the sea and slammed into Xander's side. He was thrown off balance which gave me a chance to break free. I shrugged off his hold and rushed to the side of the boat where I dove into the water.

"Miriam!" I heard Xander scream before the rush of water blocked out all sound.

The water below the surface was a swirling mix of small whirlpools and the shadows of the rocks. I could see barely ten feet in front of me, but the outline of the Sălbatic was clear. His body stretched down beyond my sight, but I could see a whirlpool lay in that direction.

Sălbatic submerged his entire body and floated in front of me. His bright eyes illuminated the small area around us, casting long shadows over the moving water.

When he spoke the sounds were in my head rather than in the water. *"I cannot begin to count the years since I last saw a half Mare fae like myself."* My eyes widened slightly as he slipped around me, encompassing me in his lithe body. His clawed hands grasped my shoulders. They were as cold as death. His chuckle vibrated the water around us. *"You are surprised, cousin, but you should not be, for my form is the many and yours is the few."* The creature reached up and grasped one of the long strands of my floating hair. He closed his eyes and sniffed it. *"Such a wonderful scent. Your soul must be beautiful."* My captor floated in front of me, completing his twining of me within his body. He opened his arms and smiled at me. *"Let me see it."*

I gasped and my eyes widened as I felt a sudden pull from within me. A bright blue light floated outward from my body and hovered a foot in front of me. The blue light formed into a transparent figure of me.

My vision blurred, or rather, it doubled. I could see my physical body staring at the blue me, and I could also see through the eyes of the me made of light.

Sălbatic chuckled. *"I was right. You are more beautiful than I could have imagined, and with your soul I will be whole."*

He floated over to my astral form and wrapped his arms around the me made of light. A sudden wrenching struck my heart as his arms wrapped around the other me. I felt like I was being crushed to death as an unbearable pressure pressed against my entire body. My heart quickened to a speed that it couldn't maintain for very long as my astral figure was absorbed into the creature's body.

A splash above us made him whip his head back and look up. I pushed through the pain and followed his gaze to see Xander kick through the water toward us. In both his hands was the glowing blade of Bucephalus. He drew back his arms and cut through the water at the snake body that surrounded me.

Sălbatic hissed at him and drew back, leaving my astral form behind. The light snapped back into my body like a stretched rubber band that was released. I took in a deep breath, and with it a mouthful of water.

Xander swam in front of me and grasped one of my shoulders. His bright green eyes studied me. I set my hand atop his and managed a weak smile. He nodded and returned his attention to our furious foe.

Sălbatic floated a mere ten feet away from us. His snake-like body slithered behind him like an impatient pet. *"You will pay for interfering, mortal.*

His snake half swam up above our heads and rushed down to crack its heavy body against Xander's head. Xander's wings burst from his back and he blocked the blow with the strong leather and bone. He pushed the serpent body away and cut the water with his sword. His blade cut a

ISLAND OF THE DRAGON

deep gash into Sălbatic's body. Red blood poured from the wound and stained the water.

Sălbatic roared and rushed Xander with his clawed hands outstretched. Xander lifted his sword and blocked the blow. Sălbatic shoved his face into Xander's and snarled at him. *"You may wound me, mortal, but I cannot die."*

Xander grinned and pushed him away. He swiped his sword in front of him, slicing a long cut along Sălbatic's torso. The creature let out a scream and sank back into the dark depths of the water. Xander turned around and swam over to me where he wrapped an arm around my waist and kicked us to the surface.

I took in a big gulp of air as we broke through the surface beside the boat. Tillit and Magnus pulled me inside as Xander followed behind me. I flopped onto the deck like a caught fish and rolled onto my back. My clothes were soaked and my body ached.

Xander knelt beside me and looked me over. "Are you unhurt?"

I sat up and nodded. "Yeah," was my hoarse reply.

"You were down there long enough to be married and have some little fishes," Tillit teased me.

Alice studied me with narrowed eyes. "And yet Sălbatic let you live."

I coughed out some water and shook my head. "He. . .he said he wanted to use me to be whole. I think he tried to use my soul to do that."

Magnus arched an eyebrow. "Make himself whole? What in the seas is that supposed to mean?"

I shrugged. "I don't know, but he said he was just like me, a half mare fae."

"Your cousin has a strange way of showing affection," Tillit commented as he turned to Alice. "So how did the vampires ever get past that thing without Xander's sword?"

"Vampires have souls that are unlike the rest of us, so when they passed Sălbatic didn't rise to plunder theirs," she explained. She returned her attention to me and furrowed her brow. "Though they always thought Sălbatic ate his victims."

"I guess I'm just one of the lucky ones," I commented as I climbed to my shaky legs. The water around us was calm but for the crashing of the rocks.

That is, until Thatch pointed at the starboard side. "The blood!"

We all looked at where he pointed. The water was stained with blood, and from that blood rose the gashed figure of Sălbatic. Gone was his handsome majesty and in its place was a blood-drenched fiend with sharp teeth. His clawed hands were balled into fists at his sides as he glared daggers at us.

"She is mine!" he screamed in our heads. The sound reverberated in our skulls and all of us but Thatch and Xander clutched our heads between our hands.

Sălbatic raised one of his claws. A column of bloodied water as wide as I was tall shot up and arched toward us. Xander leapt in front of me and raised Bucephalus above his head. The water crashed down on the sword sending blood and water spray everywhere.

Xander gritted his teeth as the pressure pushed down on him. He was forced onto one knee as the column kept gushing from the water.

Magnus whipped his head to Alice. "Get the clothes!"

She stared at him blankly for a moment before a sly smile slipped onto her lips. "Aye aye, captain!"

Together the pair untied the ropes that held our clothing on the lowest sail post. Magnus tied their tops together with a short rope of which he grabbed the untied end. Alice drew out a small throwing knife from her boot and nodded.

Magnus stepped up to the side of the ship and raised the rope above his head. He swung it around which drew the tied clothes off the deck and into the air above him.

"Watch the winds for me, bonny lass!" he shouted at Alice.

She studied the winds for a short moment before her eyes widened. "Now!"

Magnus released the rope and the clothing flew out over the water beside the column and toward our foe. Alice threw her knife and sliced through the ropes that held the 'bags' shut. The paper vampires flew out and rushed the first thing they saw, Sălbatic. He swam back and dropped his hand to throw up a guard in front of him. The paper vampires splattered against the wall of water and sank out of sight.

The column stopped its never-ending attack on our ship. Xander fell forward and his sword clattered to the deck beside him. I grabbed his shoulders to keep him upright and heard a roar from across the water.

Sălbatic flung up both his hands. Another column, twice as wide as the first, flew from the water and sped toward us.

My eyes narrowed. I stood and held up my own hands toward the column. A brilliant blue light erupted from my palms and formed a large wall over the entire side of the ship. I winced as the water hit my wall hard and kept pounding on it.

Sălbatic slithered toward us, his blue eyes ablaze with fury. The closer he came the greater the pressure against my wall. He reached the side of the boat and leaned toward me. All that separated us was a few short feet and the chaos of our dueling powers.

His eyes caught mine. I could feel his hypnotic power invade my mind. My eyebrows crashed down as I narrowed my eyes at him. "Not this time, ugly!"

I shoved my wall forward. The change in position meant the spray from the unceasing water flew back and into

its master. Sălbatic's eyes widened and he threw up his arms to protect himself from his own creation.
 I dropped to one knee and dipped my hand in the water. My familiar, the cute water dragon rose from the surface as a leviathan that cast its shadow over my foe. Its bright blue eyes glared at Sălbatic as the half-fae dropped his hands. He gaped at my monstrosity.
 I grinned. "Get 'em, boy."
 My dragon roared and lunged at Sălbatic. The Mare fae screamed and dove beneath the surface with my dragon close at his back. They disappeared into the dark depths of the bottomless water. I felt a strange tug and pulled my hand out of the water. I wasn't sure what happened, but I had a feeling it was done.

CHAPTER 12

My companions came up behind me, Xander included, and peered over the side. Tillit glanced at me and jerked his head toward the water. "Did it eat him?"

I wrapped my arms around myself as I looked into the dark depths. "I hope not."

Tillit arched an eyebrow. "Why?"

"Because I could've turned out like that."

Xander set his arms on my shoulders and smiled down at me. He looked exhausted. "

I shrugged. "I couldn't have done it without you guys distracting-" A sudden pain hit me in the head. It was like being struck by a hard hammer that dug deep into my skull. I cried out and clutched my head in both my hands as I swayed from side-to-side.

Xander cradled me against his chest. "Miriam! What is it?"

I clenched my teeth and shook my head. The pain faded enough for me to cast my gaze to Xander. "Headache," I hissed.

"Is that it?" Alice spoke up.

Tillit glanced at her and frowned. "She had one the last time she saved our skins with her magic, so don't go throwing it out like it's nothing to worry about." Alice's eyebrows crashed down, but she said nothing.

"Was the pain the same as before?" Xander asked me.

I steadied my legs and shook my head. "No, it was a hell of a lot worse."

"Mayhaps yer getting tired," Magnus suggested.

"I'm fine. See?" I pushed off from Xander's chest and stood on my own two feet. "It's already almost gone."

Xander pursed his lips. "But it may return. You must avoid using your powers."

I snorted. "*Now* you're telling me to not use my powers. Besides, who's the one using his sword like it's some sort of a shield?"

He picked Bucephalus off the deck and admired the glistening blade. "Bucephalus is a sword of legend with powers even I am not aware of, but my father told me that it did have the power to protect."

Tillit turned and looked across the water at the cave. "I hope you don't have to use it in there."

Our open sails pulled us through the calm waters and to the sandy beach that led to the cave opening. We hit bottom and Thatch dropped anchor before he turned to our group. "I'll remain aboard in case we need a fast escape."

"Not a bad idea. . ." I murmured as we climbed off the bow and stepped onto the wet sand.

Xander led our group of five the thirty feet to the opening. He stopped and turned to Alice. "Do the vampires mention whether the cave is protected?"

She jerked her thumb over her shoulder at the water at our backs. "With something like that who needs any more?"

"Agreed," Tillit spoke up.

Xander returned his attention to the cave and its darkness. He tore off one sleeve and picked up a piece of driftwood. Alice frowned. "We don't need a torch."

Xander stooped and picked up two rocks which he scraped together to create sparks over the cloth. "Miriam is in need of light."

Tillit rummaged through his satchel and pulled out a small vial. "As much faith as I have in my nose, I'd like to see what's coming before it gets me."

Tillit knelt beside Xander and poured the contents on the cloth. The sparks caught on the shirt like it was soaked in kerosene and soon Xander had a good fire going. He picked up the torch and glanced over his shoulder at us. "Follow me."

We entered the deep, dank darkness of the cave. I stayed close to the flickering torchlight and swept my eyes over the rough walls. Water dripped from the ceiling and left deep puddles, made through countless years, along the narrow path. I could barely walk beside Xander, and Tillit was close behind us. The captains brought up the rear, grudgingly at one another's side.

"So what exactly are we supposed to be looking for?" I whispered.

Xander pursed his lips as he swept his eyes over the cramped quarters. "I am not sure."

Tillit whipped out the ancient book of the library and thumbed through the pages. "It says something about a cherished treasure behind a-um, a wall."

I glanced over my shoulder and looked at him with a raised eyebrow. "A wall?"

He shrugged. "Well, that's not quite how it translates, but it's close enough."

"What's the word?" Alice asked him.

Tillit cleared his throat. "It says it's the Gateway to Truth."

Alice rolled her eyes. "Just like a dumb book to be using something stupid like that."

I glanced at her. "What do the vampires call it then?"

She glared at me. "The vampires weren't foolish enough to be tempting fate with Sălbatic."

Magnus chuckled. "I always knew their blood was yellow."

She whipped her head to him and narrowed her eyes. "You'll be seeing yer own if ya don't shut yer-"

"Quiet," Xander ordered them.

It was his turn to feel the wrath of the Ugly Look. "Why?"

He stopped and raised the torch in front of him. "I believe we are here."

The torchlight revealed a pair of stone doors. They were made from a rock as dark as night and reached from floor to ceiling without any signs of hinges or handles. There was only the impression of a single pair of hands with one print on one door and the other opposite it.

I pointed at the hand impressions. "Are those on the wrong side?"

Magnus arched an eyebrow. "So they are. The left is on the right and the right on the left."

I looked to Xander. "Did the ancient dragons look a little different than you do now?"

He shook his head. "I am not sure, but I have never heard tales of their hands being on the opposite side as ours."

"But they used to be bigger, didn't they? Maybe they switched hands later, too," I suggested.

"Perhaps," Xander murmured as he studied the doors. He handed the torch to me and stepped up to the entrance. The hand impressions were the perfect height to lay one's hands inside them. Xander lay his hands over the tops of the imprints, first crossing his arms so they matched and then using the opposite, always making sure to use both hands at the same time. Nothing happened.

Xander turned to Tillit. "What does the book tell us?"

Tillit scanned the pages. "It says here that that which is two can open the door."

Xander returned his attention to the door and pursed his lips. "A dragon lord." He raised his hands and set them into the molds again. Still nothing happened. He dropped his hands and looked up at the doors. "What are we missing..."

Magnus folded his arms across his chest and frowned. "I was at least expecting a trap."

Alice jabbed him in the arm and glared at him. "Don't tempt the gods."

Xander looked over his shoulder at our resident sus scholar and set his left hand over its corresponding imprint. "Must something else be done? An incantation or a turn?"

Tillit shook his head. "I can't find-" I hissed and grabbed my shoulder.

Everyone turned to me, including Xander who dropped his hands to his sides. "What is it?" he asked me.

I shook my head as I looked at my shoulder. "I-I don't know. It just burns."

Xander stepped up to me and pulled down my sleeve to reveal my shoulder. The Mark on my shoulder placed there so many months before glowed with a yellow light. He furrowed his brow. "The Mark can only be summoned when I am in danger."

"Maybe that's part of a trap," Magnus suggested.

"Or maybe it has something to do with what's behind that wall," Alice spoke up.

Tillit shook his head. "I'm going to take a guess and say it *is* the wall. See?" He pointed at the hand print on the left side. The indent glowed with a soft yellow light.

My eyes widened. "They're the same light."

Xander lifted my right hand and smiled at me. "Shall we?"

I shrugged. "Why not?"

Xander led me over to the door, and together we raised our opposite hands, he his left and I my right. The same light appeared in Xander's hand print, and mine brightened until I had to turn my face away and squint to look at it.

A rumble came from the wall. I felt the hand print and wall slide backward away from me. The wall split in half and the two pieces slipped into their adjoining walls. A wave of dust blew over us, choking me with its dryness and the smell of decay.

Xander stepped forward and peered inside. "By all the gods. . ." I heard him whisper.

Tillit waved his hand in front of his face and coughed. "The gods have a dry sense of humor."

The dust cleared enough that I could see into the darkness that lay beyond the wall. By the light of Tillit's torch I was able to glimpse a wide aisle. On either side of the walkway stood a half dozen large stone sarcophagus, making the total an even dozen. They were grouped into pairs set close to one another so that one could hardly squeeze between them.

Alice walked up to my side with Magnus on hers and frowned. "That's it? A bunch of tombs? Are we supposed to rob them or something?"

Magnus shook his head. "Not I. Tis bad luck."

Alice snorted. "Not in my experience."

I walked up to one of the sarcophagi and brushed my hand over the lid. The dust slid away and, though time had taken its toll, a raised stone banner colored with yellow paint was revealed. There were no other markings.

I turned to my companions. "Who are they?"

ISLAND OF THE DRAGON

Xander walked past me and to the back wall. The curved wall was as smooth as glass, but rather than a reflective surface there was a long mural. The scene was that of a city of white stone surrounded by a thick forest of tropical trees. Towers rose up from among tall houses and pierced the bright blue sky of flying birds and floating clouds. The birds flew over roofs and into the thick canopy of the lush rain forest.

The centerpiece of the painting was a stone castle. It had six towers connected by parapets and surrounded by a garden of fountains and brilliant-colored flower. In the foreground-most parapet stood six couples. The couples, each having a man and woman, faced each other. The detail was so great that I could make out their primitive gray clothing down to the bone broaches.

Curved as it was across the entire back wall, it created a panorama effect like a modern camera. I felt like I was stepping into the picture as I moved to stand by Xander's side. "Wow. . ." I whispered. My attention was caught by the castle and its towers. I furrowed my brow. "Doesn't that look like-"

"The High Castle," Xander confirmed.

"I think I see some writing up there," Magnus spoke up as he pointed at the top border.

A banner stretched the whole distance of the mural, and within its borders was written some words in the same tongue as that of the Mallus Library book.

Xander set his palm against the painting and swept his eyes over the strange letters. "To have Euclid here. . ."

"Step aside and let me have a crack at it," Alice ordered him as she dragged Magnus up to the picture.

"I might be able to help," Tillit spoke up as he sidled up to the other side of Magnus.

Alice leaned forward to stare across her captive at the sus. "You can read?"

Tillit paused in his perusing and his face fell. "Is it the face? Is that why it's so unbelievable that Tillit can read?"

I covered my mouth to hide my snicker. "A little."

"A lot," Alice quipped as she studied the wall.

Tillit sighed and resumed his perusing of the pictures and words. "Dragons. . .power. . .union. . ." he muttered.

Magnus glanced at Alice. "What do ya make of it?"

She glared at the words before she turned her face away. "Nothing. It's gibberish."

I studied the people in the scene and half-turned to look at the sarcophagus. "I'm guessing it's not just a coincidence that there are twelve coffins here and twelve people in this picture."

"Very doubtful," Xander agreed.

Tillit let out a low whistle. "Well I'll be."

Alice frowned. "You'll be something if ya don't tell us what you found out."

Tillit turned to our group and his eyes were as big as saucers. "The writing's a eulogy to them-" he nodded at the sarcophagi, "-and kind of a celebration."

I arched an eyebrow. "A celebration of what?"

"The union of dragons and humans."

CHAPTER 13

I and the rest of our group blinked at him. "Come again?" I spoke up.

He half-turned back to the mural and swept his arm over the scene. "This-all of this-is a view of a city where humans and dragons lived together. They not only lived together but-" his eyes flickered to Xander and me, "-they even married."

Alice scoffed. "Everyone knows dragons and humans have never lived together. We've always been at war."

Tillit grinned. "Then I'm about to rewrite history because that-" he pointed at the banner with the words, "-and this-" he held up the book, "-are both saying that they did. It was a really long time ago, by my counting at least twenty thousand years, but they shared cities and fields and everything. This-" he lay his palm on the mural, "-this was the first city. The first one to have the union."

"So what's the big deal?" I spoke up. "I mean, they shared a city and they might have married, but you make that sound like it's huge."

"It is," Xander replied. His lips were pursed as his eyes studied the bannered words. "It has always been tradition that dragons and humans cannot live side-by-side, excluding the Maidens."

Tillit grinned and gestured behind us. "Speaking of Maidens, say hello to the first ones."

I glanced over my shoulder at the sarcophagus and blinked at the stone coffins. "*Them*?"

He nodded. "Yep. They weren't from your world, but they *were* the first brides for the six leaders of the dragons. Princesses given to princes."

"But what made them do it?" I asked him.

Tillit glanced between the open book in his hands and the banner. "It says here, and some of it is up there, that both parties wanted to unite their powers to avoid a 'weakening,' or something like that."

I raised an eyebrow. "Weakened what?"

"A weakened line," Tillit revealed as he tapped on a page in the book.

I sidled up beside him and looked over his shoulder. A picture on the page showed two halves to a circle. One half was filled in with green coloring and showed a single white leathery wing. The other half was white and showed green stars.

I pointed at the star half. "What's that mean?"

"It's a generally accepted representation of magic," Tillit explained. He looked up at Xander. "So this shows that the dragons needed humans to grant them their strength, and humans needed dragons to give them their magic."

Xander lowered his head and stared hard at the floor. "They sought the same as my forefathers, to prevent the destruction of their line."

ISLAND OF THE DRAGON

Tillit shook his head. "It's worse than that. These dragons and humans joined together to stop the destruction of their *races*."

A hush fell over our group. My eyes widened and my mouth dropped open. "The dragons don't just need Maidens, they need *humans*."

Tillit nodded. "That's what it looks like. I guess that explains why they're not as big as they used to be, or why the humans don't do magic like they used to."

"Get out of the way!" Alice snapped as she shoved Tillit and me away from the wall. "Let me have a try. You probably read it wrong."

Tillit bowed to her, but his eyes flickered to Magnus as a sly grin danced across his lips. "She's your perfect match, captain." The stoic old sea captain studied the frantic woman, but said nothing.

"So all of this means what?" I persisted.

Xander raised his eyes to the mural and pursed his lips. "We are the source of our own destruction."

Magnus nodded. "Aye. The Great War and all its foolish little battles. I guess we're all of us the worse for it."

I furrowed my brow. "But my old world doesn't have dragons and humans are just fine, so does it only work one way?"

"Does your world contain magic?" he asked me.

My face fell. "No. . ."

Tillit rubbed his stubby chin. "So dragons need humans to retain their powers, and humans need dragons to

Alice growled and threw down her arms. "Blast it all, but the damn sus is right."

Tillit grinned and puffed out his ample chest as he clapped the book shut. "Of course Tillit is right. Tillit can read."

I wrinkled my nose and glanced at Xander. "This world hasn't really done much in that time, has it?"

"There has been too much war to progress," Xander pointed out.

I turned to the stone sarcophagus and pursed my lips. "So these are the first of me."

"And the first of my line," Xander added.

I furrowed my brow and looked back to my dragon lord. "But I thought this whole Maiden thing didn't start until five thousand years ago."

Tillit tapped on the cover of the book. "It says here in this history that the Maiden ritual fell out of favor after five thousand years and that the dragons forgot their heritage. They attacked the humans seven thousand years ago."

Xander arched an eyebrow. "Why had you not read that chapter to us earlier?"

Tillit shrugged. "I thought it was ancient history, but not *that* ancient."

I looked at the tense faces around me. "So what now? I mean, this isn't the power the book warned us about, is it?" I swept my eyes over the dry room. "And I don't see any water, either."

Tillit studied the mural and stroked his chin. "I wonder where this is."

Alice's eyes flickered over the picture. She did a double take and her eyes widened. "That's Ealand of Reod Fyr!"

All of us glanced from her to the painting. I tilted my head to one side and furrowed my brow. "How can you tell?"

She pointed at the base of the castle. "I'd stake my ship that these stones are the same ones that the barracks stand on right now."

Tillit nodded at the ground below the castle. "And that looks a lot like water, doesn't it?" There was indeed a hint of a small hint of blue color beneath the foundation of the castle.

"The book may have led us here first so that we may find this mural," Xander mused.

ISLAND OF THE DRAGON

My face fell. "Great, so this great power we're looking for is in the middle of enemy territory. Anybody have any idea how to get in there without dying?" I looked from one of my companions to the other. No one spoke up. I sighed. "Even better..."

"Let us return to the boat and gather our thoughts in the daylight," Xander suggested.

We turned away from the ancient graves and mural, and walked back down the tunnel. The mood among our small group was somber. For my part I was stuck thinking about the barracks problem and the revelation that humans were a necessary part of dragons. It made so much sense, what with the few dragons with magical powers and the dragon lords' decision to restart the Maiden ritual.

Thinking of the union of humans and dragons reminded me we had our own current union problem. Magnus and Alice walked side-by-side and cuff-to-cuff, but not hand-in-hand. The only interaction was the occasional tug on the chain by one or the other.

I sidled up to them. "Where exactly did you two agree to get married?"

Magnus puffed out his chest and grinned. "On the best ship on the seas."

Alice nodded. "Aye, and he never showed up to my ship."

Magnus whipped his head to her and frowned. "The best ship is the Blå Engel."

Alice stopped and stuck her face into his and growled. "The Rache is the finest!"

"The Blå Engel!"

"The Rache!"

I slipped between them and held up my hands. "Wait a sec. Let me get this straight. You two thought the wedding was going to take place on *your* ship, and you didn't bother to check the other to see if that's where they were?"

The captains paused in their bickering and stared blankly at one another. "You were waiting for me on yer ship?" Magnus asked her.

"And you were waiting for me on yers?" she returned.

I shook my head. "I take back what I said earlier. You two aren't a married couple, you're a couple of children." The pair turned their hard eyes on me. I stepped back with my hands raised in front of me. "Come on, you guys know it's true. Who else wouldn't bother to actually *look* for their intended?"

"That is enough," Xander called out. Tillit and he stood ten feet ahead of us and looked back at our squabbling little group.

I scuttled my argument and scurried to Xander's side. We three walked on with the pair following behind. I glanced over my shoulder at them. They didn't look at each other, but their hands were clasped. I smiled and faced ahead.

We exited the cave and found the boat still anchored where we left her. Captain Thatch stood behind the wheel, but he faced the opposite direction. His attention lay on the sky and the bright sun in it.

"Sunbathing?" Magnus scolded the old sea dog as we reached the bow.

Captain Thatch whipped his head to us and grasped the wheel before he frowned at Magnus. "You're forgetting who chased us out of the bay, and that we're still stuck on the same island."

"We don't need to be worrying about them coming to us. We're coming to them," Magnus told him.

Thatch arched an eyebrow. "Come again?"

"We need to move in as close to the barracks as the sea will allow," Xander explained.

Our captain furrowed his brow and stroked his gray beard. "I might know a good place to land, and a way to sneak past them barracks."

ISLAND OF THE DRAGON

Alice paused in climbing in the boat and stared hard at him. "How do you know a way to get in when *I* don't even know?"

He grinned. "Ya don't think those men in those stone walls get a little thirsty and lonely, do ya? And who better to give them some simple pleasures than old Captain Thatch. Now draw up that anchor and let's be off!"

CHAPTER 14

We sailed out of the Stáncarras of Whyte and followed the coast to the far side of the island. The high cliffs sank low until their gentle hills slipped into the sea. A wild rain forest grew up its hillside and covered the island like a green carpet.

Far up the hill near the top I glimpsed a faint gray structure of massive blocks. Thatch lifted his gaze to the same building and pursed his lips. "That's the barracks. We'll be avoiding them."

"So do the weard get special perks for living in the barracks?" I wondered.

Alice nodded. "Aye. They rule the island. Nobody can lay a finger on them, and anyone who tries-well, let's just say they only get to try once."

"What about the envoys they send beyond the island?" Xander asked her.

ISLAND OF THE DRAGON

She frowned. "The Red Dragons don't go off the island except to fish."

"One of them took a long detour and ended up on the other side of the continent," Tillit quipped.

"He was the same who commanded the Red Dragons at the Rising Phoenix," Xander added.

Alice furrowed her brow. "So that's where Drake's been. That son of a naga would be the first one to break the rule."

"What can you tell us about this Drake?" Xander wondered.

She shrugged. "Just that he's trouble. He appeared out of nowhere about five years ago with a lot of gold and connections. I never could figure out where any of that came from. The weard see him as their leader now and he pretty much runs the island. I'm surprised he left it."

"Mayhaps he wants more than just the island," Magnus suggested.

Xander gazed out on the far-off barracks and pursed his lips. "Perhaps. Do you know his age?"

Alice shook her head. "No, but from the tales I've heard I'd say he's hardly older than yer Maiden."

Tillit rubbed his chin. "Curiouser and curiouser. How would a young dragon like that get to be the head of an entire island in only a few years?"

I cringed. "You don't think he found what we're looking for, do you?"

"We shall see," Xander replied.

We drifted up to the beach that lay far beneath the barracks and our boat was well hidden by the countless trees. Thatch tossed the anchor off the boat before he turned to us with a grin. "I'll be going on this hunting trip with you. The way into the hill isn't easy to find, and once yer in it's even easier to get lost."

"'Into the hill?'" I repeated

He winked at me. "You'll see."

We hopped ashore and allowed Thatch to lead us into the dense jungle. There was no path to follow, only a wilderness of wide-leafed bushes and thick-trunked tropical trees that hid the sun with their foliage.

I followed close behind Alice which was a mistake. She pushed aside and released so many branches I thought I was going to end up with wooden teeth. "Could you mhmph." Another branch had whacked me in the face.

Alice paused with a branch pushed away from her and turned to me with a sly grin on her face. "Cat got yer tongue?"

"No, a dog," I quipped as I pulled bark out of my teeth. "So could you stop letting go of those branches before you bark up the wrong-" She released the branch.

This time I was prepared and ducked. My foot slipped on the wet vegetation and flew out from beneath me. I fell backwards, but Xander caught me under the arms before I hit the ground.

I glared at Alice. "What the-" My eyes widened and I pointed at the foliage. "What's that?"

Everyone followed where I pointed. A large stone block stuck out of the brush. It was as white as snow and carved to a perfect square. Xander stepped forward and brushed the countless ages of moss and dirt from its top. He revealed an intricately carved column base with figures so worn only their humanoid outlines remained. I did notice some of them sported wings behind them.

Magnus swept his eyes over the area and frowned. "I don't recall the port ever reaching this far."

"It wasn't Boldwela that stood here. It was another place, something so old nobody knows what it was," Thatch told us.

Alice's eyes widened. "The city of the ancients."

Thatch shrugged. "As good a name as any. The barracks is a part of it, so that's why we can use what's left behind to get to it."

ISLAND OF THE DRAGON

I furrowed my brow. "What was left behind?"

Our guide took a step forward and jerked his head up the path. "Follow me and be quick about it. I'm not getting any younger, ya know."

Thatch led us up a ruined cobblestone path. Now aware of what lay in the thick jungle, I could make out foundations of houses and even some crumbling walls. Toppled columns lay partially hidden among bushes and large trees.

We reached an open area where a large round tub in the middle signified it was once a square with a fountain. Large stone steps opposite where we entered led higher up the hill, but Thatch turned right and moved to stand before the wall to the right of the stairs. He drew aside a curtain of vines and revealed a tunnel. At one point the walls had been bricked, but the bricks now lay in small pieces on the ground and what was revealed were rough dirt and rocks.

A bundle of torches lay just inside the tunnel. Thatch stooped and picked up one of them which he then lit with a match.

"Torches?" Xander asked him.

Thatch turned to us and tapped his temple. "These eyes aren't getting any younger, and a good smuggler doesn't leave anything behind."

"I'll take one of those," I spoke up.

"And me," Tillit added.

Thatch shook his head. "Can't risk it. There's a lot of dry timber further in and a single flicker from one of these would send us to the Seaman's Paradise."

"'Seaman's Paradise?'" I repeated.

"Whatever comfortable afterlife you believe in," he explained.

Alice wrinkled her nose as some of the smoke hit her. "I haven't smelled something this bad since a mathair shuigh tried to drag me into the sea."

I glanced at Xander. "I think I need a full-time translator for this conversation."

"An eight-tentacled creature that resides in the shallow waters off Cayden's realm," he told me.

Alice snorted. "It wasn't in the shallow waters that I found this monster."

"Stop yer whining and get along behind me," Thatch commanded us.

We followed our irascible guide into the dank, dark tunnel. Xander stayed by my side as we walked deeper and deeper into the mountain. We walked through the smell from his torch, and I was forced to clap my hand over my nose.

"How much farther?" I mumbled through my plugged nose.

Thatch looked over his shoulder and grinned at us. "Not much farther, but watch yer step. These tunnels are full of-ah!" His foot caught in a hole and he fell face forward onto the ground.

The torch tumbled out of his hand and rolled into one of the puddles of water. The flame hissed as it met a watery end, as did our light. The world around us fell into a darkness so complete I couldn't see my nose.

I screamed as a strong pair of arms wrapped around me. "I have you," came Xander's voice from the darkness.

"Could you tell me that *before* you grab me?" I snapped.

There came the crunch of footsteps on the gravel and a groan from Thatch. "Damn stupid digging rats. . ." he mumbled.

"It's not broken," Magnus spoke up.

I heard a grunt from Thatch and then a sharp hiss as he plopped back onto the ground. "No good. It might be sprained."

"We'll carry you out," Magnus offered.

"Don't worry about me," Thatch assured him. "You just get on going down that tunnel until you reach a fork. Take the right one. That'll lead you where you need to go."

"Not if one of those weards finds you and gets the hint at what we're doing and where we went," Tillit pointed out.

Thatch chuckled. "I have enough dirt on most of those dragons that I don't think I'll be bothered, now go on before I have to use this foot to kick you."

"We'll come back for ya," Magnus promised.

"Fine, fine, now be off with you!" Thatch insisted.

We continued on with our journey, but it felt like another, darker world. I clung to Xander's arm as he guided me through the shadowed darkness. "Why can't these places have glowing rocks? Or maybe a night light?"

He stopped and there was tension in his voice. "Your wish may have been granted. Look ahead."

I squinted down the tunnel and glimpsed a faint light at the end. My heart fell into my stomach. "You don't think this goes to that Seaman's Nirvana, do you?"

"Seaman's Paradise, and no, I do not believe it does," Xander assured me.

"It doesn't flicker like candlelight, or a torch," Tillit commented.

Xander slipped his arm around my waist and held me close. "Then we shall see what this new light is."

We strode down the tunnel and in twenty yards came upon our discovery. The tunnel opened into a small, circular room with three branches opposite the one through which we entered. On the ceiling of that room hung a string of light bulbs. The string looped around the ceiling until its source disappeared into a tiny hole in the center.

Xander raised his hand to one of the bulbs and furrowed his brow. "What sorcery is this that creates light and heat without flame?"

I tilted my head back and pursed my lips.. "It's not sorcery. It's electricity."

Xander dropped his hand and looked down the tunnel with a frown on his lips. "It is forbidden for technology from your world to pass to ours."

"Pity."

ISLAND OF THE DRAGON

CHAPTER 15

We swung around and faced a dark, hidden alcove. A figure stepped from the deep shadows. My eyes widened. It was the face of the Red Dragon from so many other adventures, the one Alice called Drake.

"It is a pleasure to meet you, Ferus Draco. My name is Drake, but I have no doubt you have already learned that," he mused.

Other shadows followed him, Red Dragons with blackened fingers and dark eyes. An old man stepped up to Drake's side. He was bent with age and was attired in a ruby-red robe. His small black eyes darted over us, but stopped on Tillit.

A puff of white air snorted from Tillit's nostrils. "You're looking as decrepit as ever, Philippus," he commented.

The ancient creature frowned. "Thy mouth is as filthy as always, Tillit."

"Gentlemen, you may finish your squabbling elsewhere," Drake spoke up. He returned his attention to Xander, and there was a crooked smile on his lips as he folded his arms across his chest. "Are you not pleased, Ferus Draco? I had heard you were eager to see electricity."

Xander stepped in front of me and stretched out his arm to his side so it covered my front. His lips curled back in a snarl and he narrowed his eyes as he glared at our foe. "So this was a trap all along."

The Red Dragon shook his head. "Not *all* along. Merely since you went into the Cave of the Dragons. It was then that we convinced our old acquaintance here to lead you into my grasp."

He gestured to a passage on his left. Out of the shadows stepped Thatch.

"You dog!" Magnus screamed as he unsheathed his sword. Our foes responded by drawing their own swords.

Drake held up his hand. "Enough. Whatever efforts you put forth for revenge or to free yourselves is pointless."

Magnus narrowed his eyes at our former ally. "Not if he goes down with me."

"You snake! You sold us out for what?" Alice hissed at Thatch.

"Something your youth wouldn't understand," Thatch replied as his eyes flickered to Drake. "And speaking of that, I'll be taking what's owed to me."

Drake smiled and bowed his head. "Of course." He reached into his coat and drew out a long plume. Its feather stretched to a foot and was a dazzling display of rainbow colors that shimmered down its soft surface. The quill was half as long and ended in a sharp point. He held it out to Thatch. "One phoenix feather for your friends."

Thatch frowned as he snatched the feather from the Red Dragon. "Don't go playing the sentimental card on me, Drake. This-" he held up the feather, "-this and my youth is all I need."

ISLAND OF THE DRAGON

Drake bowed his head. "I stand corrected. Now if you will excuse us we must be going."

Thatch grabbed Drake's arm and frowned. "Nobody's taking anybody until I've seen that the goods are good."

Drake stepped back and gestured to our former ally. "As you wish."

Thatch rolled up his sleeve to expose his bare arm. He hovered the tip of the quill over his flesh for a moment before he clenched his teeth and stabbed the point deep into himself. Blood poured out of the wound, but the moment he removed the quill the blood stopped and the wound disappeared.

Other changes took place as Thatch's wrinkled skin smoothed and lightened. Scars disappeared and his gray beard changed to a dark brown color. In a few moments we were looking at Thatch as he was at his prime.

Thatch looked down at himself and grinned. "I feel like a new man, and my old self."

"Satisfied?" the Red Dragon asked him.

The young captain looked up at him and nodded. "Aye, but you won't be." Thatch spun around and grabbed the nearest weard. He lifted the guard above his head and threw the thrashing dragon into the crowd of others, knocking them down like bowling pins.

Thatch drew out a small throwing knife and whipped his head to us. "Run!"

I was half-turned toward the tunnel when Thatch threw the knife at the string of lights. Whoever had wired the electricity had obviously not been a qualified electrician because when the knife came into contact with a bulb the entire string exploded in a brilliant shower of sparks.

I raised my arms to protect myself, but Xander swept me into his arms and rushed out of the room with our friends close on our heels. The dazzling display of poor wiring allowed me to see down most of the tunnel. Thatch somehow got ahead of us and pointed at a skinny side corridor I hadn't noticed in the pitch blackness. "This way!"

With the Red Dragons regrouping and no doubt going to follow us, we reluctantly followed our former ally. He shoved us into the hole and jumped in after us.

Magnus glared at him. "Ya dirty-"

"Quiet!" Thatch hissed.

We all held our breaths as the weard passed by our hiding spot. They paused a few yards away and one of them growled. "I can't smell nothing with that damn stench."

"Thatch must have planned this from the beginning," another snarled.

"We'll follow the tunnel. They couldn't have gotten far," the first suggested.

The group hurried along. After a few moments we let out a whoosh of air. Thatch wiggled past us and deeper into the corridor. "Come on," he whispered.

Xander set me down, but grabbed my hand and led me after our traitorous guide. We followed Thatch for half a mile until the way opened to another round room with two passages, not counting our own entrance. The tunnel to our right had natural light at the end. More electric lights lit up the ceiling, but there was no sign or sound of our pursuers.

Thatch turned to us and grinned. "Not bad, eh?" Magnus marched forward and punched Thatch in the cheek. Thatch stumbled back and cupped his face as he chuckled. "I'll take that as a 'yes.'"

"Ya damn fool! Ya could've gotten us all killed with yer show!" Magnus growled.

Thatch drew out a dagger from his belt and pointed it at us. With his other hand he pulled a small metal ball from his pocket. "To be perfectly honest it wasn't quite a show. You see, a lot of people want to see you dead, and they want to do it themselves. That makes you pretty valuable on the Deep Market."

Magnus narrowed his eyes and clenched his teeth. "Ya damn scoundrel! Ya mean to sell us to the highest bidder!"

Thatch chuckled. "You always were quick, Magnus. That's why I made you captain, and that's why I have this." He raised the metal ball in front of him. "That Red Dragon was nice enough to give me a bit of Dragon's Bane in case I had to 'convince' you to go into these passages."

Tillit lifted his nostrils and sniffed the air. His eyes flickered to Xander and a sly smile slipped onto his lips. "Smells like trickery."

Xander leapt at Thatch. The captain stumbled back and threw the ball at my dragon lord. The ball hit him in the chest and burst open. An acidic mist filled the narrow passage. I choked on the horrific smell as the sounds of scuffling came through the thick fog. The air cleared enough that I could see Captain Thatch pinned to the ground by Xander and Tillit.

Magnus dragged Alice up to his old mentor and glared down at him. "Ya might be young again, Thatch, but yer aim is as bad as ever."

"His aim was not the problem," Xander commented as Tillit and he lifted Thatcher onto his feet. He turned to us and revealed the wet spot on his front. "The ball did not contain Dragon's Bane, but a simple mixture of sulfur and dry ice."

Tillit grinned and tapped the side of his nose. "The nose doesn't lie."

Magnus returned his attention to Thatch and frowned. "Ya got what ya deserved. A lie for a liar."

A crooked grin slipped onto Thatch's lips. "You may have got me, but I've got my years back."

Alice picked up the dagger Thatch had dropped and glanced between the sharp blade and Thatch's throat. "We can fix that."

Magnus lay his hand on Alice's wrist and pushed the dagger down as he shook his head. "As much as I'd like to have this dog drowned in the bay, that wouldn't be the justice an old captain deserves."

She sneered at him, but tucked the dagger into her belt. "On this island that *is* justice."

"As touching as this talk of murdering someone is, I think we need to get out of here as soon as possible," Tillit spoke up.

As if one cue there came a noise of dozens of feet running down the passage in our direction. The owners of the feet appeared, large weard with murder in their eyes and swords in their hands.

"Run!" Xander yelled.

ISLAND OF THE DRAGON

CHAPTER 16

Too late. Our escape was cut off as a few of the weard flew over our heads and landed down-passage from where we stood. We were trapped. The chief Red Dragon stepped from their midst and smiled at us. "It seems you had but a brief respite from fate, Ferus Draco, but we really must be going. There is something I wish to show you." Xander curled his lips back in a snarl as he narrowed his eyes. The Red Dragon wagged his finger at my dragon lord. "None of that now. You would not wish for your precious fae to be harmed, would you?" Several of the sword-wielding dragon men took a step toward me.

A cry of pain from Thatch made us all look at him. His face scrunched up as he clutched his stomach. Something like thousands of tiny pins shifted beneath his clothes. He threw his head back and screamed as they broke through, revealing themselves to be feather quills. Bright feathers the colors of the rainbow sprouted out of the ends of the hollow stems.

Thatch lifted his hands and his eyes widened as they transformed into long claws. He whipped his head to Drake who stood nearby with a sly smile on his face. "W-what have you done to me?"

The Red Dragon shook his head. "I have done nothing but give you what you desired, eternal life. Unfortunately-" he strode over to Thatch and knelt on one knee before the disfigured man as Thatch's face elongated into a beak, "-that wish comes with a price. The phoenix is the only creature in our world that is immortal, so in order to become immortal yourself you must become one of them."

"No!" Thatch screeched as his feet transformed into claws. He grabbed the front of the dragon's shirt. "You must help me! Change me back!"

Drake frowned and whacked his hands away before he stood. "There is no reversing this 'gift,' so bear the start of your eternal life with some dignity, will you?"

Thatch narrowed his now-golden eyes and with an ear-piercing shriek he lunged at the dragon. Some of the weard rushed forward to protect their leader. Xander, Magnus and Alice each picked up one of the distracted guards and threw them into their comrades while Tillit grabbed my hand and pulled me toward the passage with the light.

Our other three companions soon joined us, but we weren't followed. Thatch was giving all he got against Drake and the weard. He was now more bird than man-dragon, with feathers covering his body and his feet split into three talons. His terrible screeches vibrated my eardrums and the walls. Debris fell from the ceiling and the walls and ground began to shake. Large rocks began to litter the ground behind us and threatened to block off the tunnel at our backs.

ISLAND OF THE DRAGON

Magnus slid to a stop and turned to face the fierce battle between bird and dragon. "Captain! Come with us!"

Thatch turned to us and smiled. "God speed, Captain Magnus, and may the winds ever be in yer favor." He leaned back and let loose a harsh shriek that shook the earth so bad I clung to the walls.

Alice grabbed Magnus's shoulders. "Get back!"

She pulled him backward just as the ceiling crashed down. The passage was filled with choking dust that filled our lungs and made us cough. I waved my hand in front of my face and squinted into the dirty fog. Magnus stood before a huge pile of stones that blocked the way we came.

Xander walked up to the old captain and set a hand on Magnus's shoulder. "I am sorry about your friend."

Magnus shook his head. "Twas his own doing. I expect he made his bed a long time ago, and now he's lying in it." The old captain raised his eyes to Xander and pursed his lips. "I'm just sorry ya got dragged into it, Yer Lordship."

Tillit looked down the path available to us. It was a roughly-hewn corridor littered with puddles and mud. There were a few offshoots on either side. "We need to get going. It didn't take those Red Dragons long to find us the first time and they're sure to have a surprise waiting for us a third time if we don't get out of here quick."

Xander turned away from the pile of rocks and strode over to me where he grasped my upper arms. "Are you okay?"

I managed a weak smile and nodded. "I'm alive. I think."

He returned my smile and guided me down the path toward the bright light. "We shall keep you in that state."

Xander couldn't keep his promise for long as out from the side passages came hordes of red-sashed dragons. My dragon lord pulled me behind him and grabbed the shirt of the first foe. He lifted him up and tossed him into his comrades, but others passed them and swarmed us. Magnus and Alice hurried up, cutlasses in hand, and joined in the fray in the cramped quarters. The passage was so narrow that none of the Red Dragons could get past us, but we couldn't get past them.

I was pushed back as Xander retreated a step and my foot slipped into a deep puddle. The little pools of water were like stepping stones to our point of freedom. I stooped and dipped my hand into the cool, sludgy water and grimaced, but focused my eyes on the many puddles beneath the feet of our foes. Little dragons as thin as snakes burst from my puddle and leapt like dolphins into the next ones, growing larger and multiplying.

They slipped beneath the feet of the Red Dragons and came up with their wide, teeth-filled mouths open. My little pets latched onto the legs and arms of the men, and in some cases the family jewels, and slammed them down face-first into the rocky floor. There were dozens of screams of pain and terror as the men tried to grab the little dragons, but found themselves with their hands only full of water.

"Now!" Xander shouted as he grabbed my arm.

I yanked myself free of his grasp. "Don't move me or they'll get free!"

Magnus and Alice hurried past us and kicked and slashes their way through our preoccupied foes. Tillit drew up beside us and nodded at Xander's sword. "Give her that so she can drag it from puddle to puddle."

Xander dipped the tip of his sword into my puddle and soaked the surface with water that dripped back down into the puddle. I gingerly climbed my way up the sword, keeping contact with the water. I was able to stand and, with Tillit in front of me and Xander at my side, we rushed forward. The tip of the sword never left the wet ground so that my little dragons remained active in their duties.

We just barely left them behind and the exit was only twenty yards off when I was hit with an excruciating pain. The pain split my head in two. My vision blurred and I stumbled into the wall on my right. Xander swept me into his arms and ran down the passage. I let out a scream as my splitting headache turned into a full-body wracking pain. A bright blue light burst from my hands and shot upward. The pair of lights twirled around each other and called forth my familiar water dragons from the water around us. The creatures thrashed around like disobedient children, knocking into Xander and sending us both into the wall. Xander hit the rocks hard and fell to the floor. I landed on top of him.

My head ached like someone had hit me with an ax and I still couldn't see very well, but I could see Xander's pale face near mine. My eyes widened as I saw blood pour from a small wound along his temple. I climb to a seated position and, working through the pain, shook his shoulders. "Xander? Xander!"

His eyes flew open and zoomed in on me. "Miriam. Are you unhurt?"

I couldn't suppress a snort. "I should be asking you that, but come-" One of the flailing bodies of the water dragons slammed into the wall to my left.

Xander grabbed the back of my head and forced us both to the ground as the other dragon dragged itself across the wall where he had just leaned.

Tillit had stopped five yards from us and faced us. "Behind you!"

I whipped my head back down the passage. My little dragons were gone so that our foes were back on their feet and had murder in their eyes. They stepped toward us, daring the wrath of my writhing dragons.

"Run!" Xander ordered him.

Tillit shook his head. "Not without you."

"You are the only one who can decipher that book! You must run and lead others to the water!" Xander insisted.

"I'm not going-" Xander threw Bucephalus at our friend and it was lodged into the ground at Tillit's feet.

"Keep that for when we meet again!" Xander promised.

Tillit plucked the sword from the ground and pursed his lips before he turned and fled down the path to the light.

Xander turned his attention to me. "Can you control your dragons?"

I clenched my teeth and shook my head. "I can't even-ah!" I was struck with another blow of pain. This was cramped up my entire body.

That last thing I saw was the shadows of the Red Dragons as they descended on us.

ISLAND OF THE DRAGON

CHAPTER 17

I woke up with a hell of a headache. My head pounded like someone had a jackhammer against my skull. I forced my eyes opened and blinked against bright electric lights. All those months with just candles and sunlight had strengthened my eyes.

After a moment I grew accustomed to the light and saw I lay in an overstuffed Victorian sofa. I sat up and found myself in an elegant living room furnished with clawed-foot tables and chairs. A large stone fireplace adorned one wall, and over its hearth hung a large portrait. The picture was of a stern-looking man in a red robe. His brushed-back hair was a shocking red color. His dark eyes seemed to stare into my soul.

Someone was staring at him. Xander stood before the hearth and looked up at the portrait.

"Xander?" I whispered as I slid off the sofa.

He didn't looked at me when he spoke. "I am sorry."

I stepped up beside him and raised an eyebrow as I studied his intense gaze. "Sorry about what?"

He turned his head toward me and caught my gaze in his own. "For involving you in my family's troubles. This feud has pulled both of us into the clutches of that-" he clenched his teeth, "-that Bestia Draconis."

I touched his arm and smiled up at him. "Partners?"

His face softened, but not when he looked back at the portrait. He furrowed his brow. I followed his gaze and frowned. "That's the Red Dragon lord, isn't it?"

He nodded. "Yes."

"The one you killed?" I persisted.

"The very one."

I crossed my arms over my chest and glared at him. "Are you going to tell me the whole truth or not? If I'm going to die I'd like to know why."

Xander sighed and pursed his lips. "You know that my mother was killed, and my father died with her, but you have not been told the whole truth about the attack." He pulled away from me and paced the floor. "The Red Dragon was of my father's generation, and therefore they chose their Maidens in the same ceremony. Unfortunately, his Maiden could not give him an heir."

My eyes widened. "She. . .she couldn't have kids?"

He nodded. "That is correct. He demanded he be given another chance at a Maiden and that the other five lords agree to open the Portal. They refused. Such a thing had never been done, and they instead suggested he wait for the next Choosing."

I arched an eyebrow. "Doesn't that take place when all the lords are dead?"

"The other lords made a concession that should he be the last he would be able to choose another Maiden," Xander told me.

I ran my hand through my hair and shook my head. "That is the stupidest thing I ever heard."

ISLAND OF THE DRAGON

"He did have the option to take a dragon bride," Xander added.

My eyes flickered up to him. "What about that whole ten-generation thing the lords were trying to do? Wouldn't taking a dragon woman at eight have messed it up?"

"It would have merely delayed the completion." He paused and turned to face me. "Truth be told my father and the others were concerned about the Red lord. He had a single-minded interest in the other world, particularly their weapons. Fortunately the Maidens were not versed in their creation, or it was believed he would have created some of them to begin a war. There was also his priests at the temple who caused unease among the others with their intense study of the portals. The other lords' refusal only increased the veracity of their study. There was fear of a revolt among them."

"Some things never change. . ." I muttered.

Xander nodded. "Yes. The supreme irony is that many of the other dragon lords and their vassals perished during the war."

I shook my head. "So he almost got what he wanted, anyway."

Xander lifted his chin and stared hard at the portrait. "Yes, but he lost it all."

"And I will find it."

We spun around to face the door. Drake stood in the doorway with a sly smile on his face. He stepped inside and closed the door behind him. "I see you are admiring my ancestor's portrait."

Xander's eyes narrowed. "Then you are of that cursed clan."

Drake bowed his head. "I am. The gentleman over the fire is my grandfather." Xander started back. Our foe chuckled. "Yes. *I* am the tenth generation."

I frowned and glanced up at Xander. "But you said his Maiden couldn't have kids."

"And he is not wrong," Drake spoke up as he circled us with that terrible smile on his lips and a darkness in his eyes. "That Maiden was infertile, but after the decision by the other dragon lords to extinguish our line he commanded his priests to look into creating a portal of his own. After a time he succeeded and-" his eyes fell on me and a sneer teased the corners of his lips, "-he brought forth one of your wretched kind with whom to procreate. My father was the product of that union, but he was unknowingly killed in the war. Fortunately, not before he produced me through another worthless Maiden brought from the other world."

I glared at him. "She was your mom."

He laughed at me. "What do I care for her? She died giving birth to me, and that was the end of that nuisance."

I crossed my arms over my chest and frowned. "You should care about all the Maidens. They're what gives you your strength."

Drake chuckled. "Maidens are merely a necessary evil, an inconvenience that may be discarded once another path to dragon purity is found."

Xander sneered at him. "Power before all."

Drake smiled and bowed his head. "A family saying I carry with relish, but this is all in the past and I care only for the present." He sidled up to Xander and studied him. "I am curious, Ferus Draco, if your power is as great as mine. Would you like to know what it is to have the full power of our ancestors? What strength runs through my veins?"

"We have seen enough of your power," Xander remarked.

Drake chuckled. "Those diversions? They were merely to entertain me while my plan was finalized."

"And you can't help but tell us that plan," I spoke up.

He bowed low and gestured to the door. "If you would follow me then I shall show you."

"Do we have a choice?" I quipped.

His smile widened. "Of course not, but if you would follow me of your own volition-" his eyes flickered to Xander, "-I may be able to make additions to your interesting story."

Xander narrowed his eyes. "What do you mean?"

"Your slander to my grandfather regarding your mother," he teased. He stepped back and opened the door. "If you would follow me."

Xander pursed his lips. I slipped my hand into his and looked into his eyes. He stared into mine and I nodded.

"Then if you would," Drake persisted.

Drake led us out into a hall much like those we previously explored with Thatch. Red-sashed dragon men lined both sides of the roughly-hewn halls every few yards and glared at us. Others leered at me. I leaned against Xander and couldn't stop myself from counting the guards. My count was up to two hundred when the path widened. A bitter scent like chlorine stung my nostrils.

We arrived at a large wooden door some ten feet tall and six feet wide. Two guards stood on either side. They were larger than the others by a head and wore black bullet-proof vests taken from my old world. At their hips were pistols.

"So are we going to face the firing squad?" I spoke up.

Drake half-turned to me with his dark smile. "With your human firearms? We have brought some over from the other side, but they are little toys compared to the power we found beneath this ancient city."

The door opened and revealed a round room that was a hundred feet deep and wide. The ceiling was domed and covered in weathered paintings. The very top was devoid of color but for a strange white blemish. The cause lay in the center of the floor. At that point was a perfectly circular hole some fifteen feet wide in circumference. Out of the hole floated a thin white mist. The smell came from the hole.

Around the perimeter of the room stood another fifty Red Dragons. They wore swords and were as tall as the pair outside. Their wings were folded against their backs and their arms at their sides. They didn't move an inch as the door was shut behind our group and Drake turned to us.

"As I promised, some *real* truth about my grandfather's intentions. You see, the day he invaded Alexandria was not to murder your dear mother." Drake stepped up to Xander and grinned. "It was to make her his own."

Xander's eyes narrowed. "His actions would still have been considered an act of war."

Drake raised his hand and smiled. "You misunderstand me. I am grateful my grandfather bungled his foolish assault on your castle and killed your mother."

Xander roared and leapt at him. Drake grabbed Xander's outstretched, clawed hands and easily grappled with my dragon lord. "As amusing as this is, Ferus Draco, I am eager to

He nodded at the guards near the door behind us. Four of them rushed forward and grabbed Xander. They tore him off our foe and pulled him back.

Drake stepped up to Xander and tilted his head to one side. "As I was saying, if you had not killed my father then my line would have been set aside in favor of any offspring from that union. Then I would no doubt have been killed as a possible usurper and would not have discovered something that will be a shining jewel that will top the crown of my illustrious family." His eyes settled on me. "You told me that the Maidens were the source of our power." He stepped to one side and gestured to the hole. "*That* is the source of our power."

Drake nodded at the guards at our backs. Three of them shoved Xander forward to the edge of the hole. The fourth grabbed me by the arms and carried me to the hole where he set me down hard on my feet.

ISLAND OF THE DRAGON

"Easy there, tiny," I growled.

A glistening light on my face caught my attention. I looked ahead and down into the hole. A hundred feet below us was a large circular room the length and width of a football field. Its ceiling, too, was domed and half the floor was made of smoothed gray river stones that circled the source of the light.

The light came from a deep pool of water that stood in the center. Darkness obscured the bottom, but the surface was illuminated with a faint white glow of light. The source of the light appeared to be the water itself which let off small wisps of steam that floated up through the hole into the room in which we stood.

Xander's eyes widened and a whispered word passed his lips. "Sæ."

CHAPTER 18

Drake joined us at the edge and grinned down at the water. "Precisely. The fabled water of our ancestors, and the true source of our strength."

"A puddle of water is the source of your strength?" I quipped.

He shook his head. "Not just a puddle of water, Maiden, but a-"

"Miriam," I corrected him.

Drake chuckled. "Perhaps not for long, but on the matter of the Sæ it is a very unique body of water. It grants to anyone who touches it the power of their ancestor. Unfortunately, it also has the effect of changing one *into* that ancestor. "

Xander frowned. "And you intend to use that power to rule the world?"

Drake bowed his head. "But of course."

I rolled my eyes. "Typical."

ISLAND OF THE DRAGON

Drake's dark eyes flickered between us. "It will be fitting for a dragon lord to kill his Maiden as this mess started with a Maiden."

Xander curled his lips back in a snarl. "I would never stoop to your level."

He stepped back and chuckled. "The Sæ will change your mind."

The three Red Dragons who held Xander tied ropes around him and grabbed me. Together we were shoved to the edge of the hole. Our toes peeked over into the abyss.

Drake swept his arm over his chest and bowed to us. "Goodbye, and may the best species win."

Xander and I were thrown through the hole. We dropped the hundred feet into the muck of the thick, sticky, yellow-colored miasma. I swam to the surface and gasped for breath. Xander did the same close to me. We swam to the wide edge of smooth-stoned floor that surrounded the entirety of the pool and climbed out. Ancient bones littered the ground and fell to dust if we even brushed against them.

I stood and wiped some of the green muck off my sleeves. That's when I heard the growl. It was a deep, guttural noise. I turned around to face the pool. Xander knelt beside the edge. His breathing was harsh and his hands grasped the floor so hard he left deep claw marks.

"Xander?" I whispered as I stepped toward him and stretched out my hand.

My eyes widened as my hand was illuminated by a blue light. I held out both hands with the palms toward me. The skin was smooth and pale. My eyes flickered left and right as my hair lightened and grew longer so that it teased my waist. The light in my hands grew brighter, but through it I saw a change in Xander.

He lifted his head and let loose an echoing roar. His clothes were shredded as his body expanded and transformed into his dragon form, but nearly twice as large as usual. I stood and rushed backwards against the wall to avoid his massive clawed hands as his tail dipped into the pool.

Drake knelt beside the edge of the hole and smiled down at us. "Now you see the true power of the Sæ. Can you imagine what chaos would ensue if I were to drop even a small bucket onto a single dragon lord city?"

I saw all too well as Xander raised himself off the smooth stones and turned his head to and fro. His bright eyes swept over the area, and in their depths I saw none of his humanity. He was a creature of pure instinct.

"I look forward to your transformation, Maiden," Drake called down to me with a chuckle. "I have heard humans were once great apes. We shall see how long you can swing against our ancestor."

Above us the Red Dragons laughed and cheered. Some bet on the winner. I imagined the odds were against me.

Xander reared his head back and gave a great, echoing cry that shook the walls. I tried to scoot along wall, but he spotted me and whipped his head in my direction to glare at me. I stopped dead in my tracks. My heart thumped against my ribs.

I swallowed the lump in my throat and took a step forward with my hands in front of me. "X-Xander, come on, this isn't you. You have to get a-" He dug his claws into the pool stones and charged me.

I shrank back and flung up my hands. A bright blue light blasted out of my palms and struck Xander in the chest. Steam rose up from him as my brilliant light burned away the miasma that covered his body. He let out a weak cry and collapsed onto the stones, cracking them beneath his great weight.

The steam rose through the hole in the ceiling and forced the Red Dragons away from the scene. One of the dragons didn't back up fast enough and was covered by the steam. His wings burst from the mist and he let loose a fierce roar before he lunged at his nearest companion.

Xander's body began to shrink, but only to half his great girth. My eyes traveled down his form and I saw his tail still lay in the pool.

I pursed my lips and rushed past him. He growled and raised himself to follow me to the edge of the pool. I turned so one side was toward him and the other to the pool. I pointed one hand at the pool and other at him. Another pulse of blue energy blasted from my hands, hitting both the pool and my charging dragon lord. The dragon was pushed back and slammed against wall. He slumped to the floor unconscious.

The pool released steam, but most of it didn't evaporate. I turned to face the horrid water and pointed both glowing hands at the liquid. Bright streams of light shot from my palms and hit the water. Great billowing columns of white steam rose up and escaped through the hole in the ceiling. Some of the fog floated away from me and hit the opposite wall. The white mist slipped into a doorway-shaped crack in the wall, revealing a hidden entrance.

A heavy fatigue hit me. I dropped my arms and stumbled back. The blue light faded, but didn't disappear. I turned around to see Xander, naked and back in his human form, spread over the ruined rocks.

I stumbled over and knelt beside him. He lay face-down, but I could see his chest moved up and down. Another roar from above us made me look over my shoulder and up at the ceiling. The rampaging Red Dragon was throwing his comrades around the large room. Some of them were fighting back trying to restrain him as his clothes burst, revealing thick, scaly muscles.

I whipped my head back to Xander and shook his shoulders. "Xander! Xander, you've got to wake up!"

His eyes fluttered open and zoomed in on me. He frowned. "Who are you?"

I smiled down at him. "Your guardian angel."

His eyes widened and he reached up a hand to cup one of my cheeks. "Miriam?"

"That's my alias, but enough talk." I grabbed one of his arms and gave a tug. "We need to get out of here."

I helped him to his feet and draped his arm over my shoulders.

I heard a roar and looked up. The Red Dragon from above was stabbed in the back by one of his comrades. The force pushed him through the hole and he disappeared into the great mist. There was a loud splash as he hit water.

My eyes widened as my heart skipped a beat. "Uh-oh. . ."

A huge shadow rose from the mist. It let out a terrific, familiar roar that shook the dome. Bits of stone fell from the ceiling and rained down upon us. The Red Dragons at the hole disappeared as they scuttled away.

Drake was the last to leave the opening. His eyes glowed a hideous red color as he glared down at us. He turned away and disappeared with the rest.

Another roar returned my attention to the large, scaly problem at hand. Wings as long as houses stretched out of the mist and a single flap blew it away to reveal my efforts at destroying the water. The deep pool was now little more than a shallow wading spot, but the Red Dragon had become immersed in the four feet that remained in the center.

I swallowed the lump in my throat and readjusted Xander's weight. "I think it's time to leave."

"Leave me here," he hoarsely whispered. "I am too heavy and will only weigh you down."

"I won't argue with that, but I'm not leaving you here to become dragon chow," I argued as I dragged him around the pool toward the hidden entrance I had seen. "Besides, you owe me a big, nice dinner for almost making *me* into chow."

ISLAND OF THE DRAGON

The dragon's eyes rested on us. It curled its lips back and revealed fangs half my height and as sharp as a well-loved dagger. I hurried along the edge of the pool with Xander stumbling along beside me.

The dragon let loose another earth-shaking roar and leaned down to snap our heads off. I flung up my free hand at the shallow water between us and the dragon. A wide, thick column of steam sprung up and hit the dragon in the face. It reared back and cried as the steam struck its sensitive eyes.

Xander lifted his head and studied me. "You are capable of controlling water from afar?"

I looked down at my hands and pursed my lips as the blue light disappeared. My dazzling, goddess-like beauty also left me, leaving me back to my old self. "I think that trick just ran out, so let's do the same and get the hell out of here."

CHAPTER 19

Together we hurried across the stones to the hidden entrance. The wall looked like any other part of the pool room, but little bits of plaster lay on the floor and some chunks of the stuff hung loose off the wall. I slammed the bottom of my fist against the wall and watched as an avalanche of plaster fell to reveal a wooden door.

"Allow me," Xander insisted as he slipped out of my arm.

He grabbed the edges of the door, gritted his teeth, and yanked backward. The ancient door fell away and revealed a long, roughly-cut passage. He tossed the door to the side as the dragon behind us roared again.

I looked over my shoulder and watched the beast climb out of the pool. It opened its tall mouth and in the depths of its throat I glimpsed the makings of a huge fireball. Xander swept me into his arms and carried me over the threshold of the secret exit. I had a great view as the dragon

ISLAND OF THE DRAGON

spit out its flaming ball of fury. The ball struck the ground ten feet behind us and melted the stone. The heat scorched my cheeks and forced me to look away.

The exit was a tunnel lined with bricks and cobwebs. The air was musty and with each pounding step Xander stirred up a small poof of dust. The walls shook as the dragon screamed its fury.

A loud crashing noise forced me to look back. The dragon was pushing its way into the tunnel, causing every loose brick around us to fall to the ground. Its girth prevented it from causing a complete collapse of the tunnel as it wiggled its way down the tunnel after us. Xander ducked and dodged the debris, losing ground as the dragon closed the gap.

The passage wound its way through the mountain for fifty yards when the musty air changed to damp. Puddles formed at our feet and the bricks fell away to reveal the moldy surface of the tunnel. A faint light appeared at the end of the path. The dragon was now only twenty feet behind us and closing.

The next moment we leapt through a mess of thick trees and vines and stumbled out on the upper side of the barracks hill. A hundred feet above us stood the imposing building, and below us lay the steamy jungle that hid the forgotten city.

We had only a few seconds to admire the view before the dragon burst from the tunnel, throwing rocks everywhere. Xander pulled me behind him as faced the beast. The creature stood and cast its shadow over us. Saliva dripped from its mouth and hit the ground with a sizzle. The claws dug deep into the earth.

We took a step back, but froze when the beast curled its lips back and growled. Those hideous eyes were focused only on us.

"Run," Xander whispered to me.

I glared at him. "Not on your life."

"Miriam, please-" The dragon swooped down and opened its gaping mouth. Xander shoved me out of its path and braced his legs against the ground as he threw up his hands.

The dragon's teeth were two feet from Xander when a dark cloud swarmed over its face. The creature drew its head back and stumbled backwards, but the cloud followed it. I climbed to my feet and squinted my eyes at the small attackers. They resembled paper bats.

"Not a bad shot, was it?" a voice spoke up.

Xander and I whipped our heads to our right. Out of the brush stepped Tillit. In one hand was his tube cannon. He shouldered the weapon and grinned at us. "You guys are always so easy to find. I just have to find the most trouble and-" he paused and swept his eyes up and down Xander. He chuckled as he drew off his long coat and threw it at our dragon lord. "My Lord, I do believe you're birthright is showing."

The mutant dragon screamed and clawed at its face. The creature turned away from us and its tail flew at us. Xander swept me off my feet and leapt over the tail as it drew it back and slammed the ground. We ran past Tillit who yelped as the dragon fired off a random ball of flame that hit the ground near him. He fired off another shot from his tube before he rushed after us.

"I hope you have a plan after my shots are out!" Tillit shouted.

I glanced over Xander's shoulder at our giant foe. The mutant dragon opened its mouth and out of its jaw erupted a huge stream of fire. The paper vampires were caught in the flames and exploded into tiny bits of cinder. The dragon raced through their remains and followed us down the hill.

"I hope that thing can't-" It opened its wings and leapt into the air, making itself airborne and cutting the distance between us in half. My face fell. "-fly. . ."

ISLAND OF THE DRAGON

It flew past us and landed with a crash thirty feet down the trail. Xander and Tillit skidded to a stop as the dragon bent down and snarled at us. Its face was married with dozens of cuts that left a trail of sludgy black blood on the ground. The creature opened its mouth and showed off the fireball developing in the back of its long throat.

Xander rushed forward and grabbed the top jaw. He slammed it down into the lower jaw and wrapped his arms around both of them, sealing the fireball. The dragon raised its head and flailed around to try to shake Xander loose. He swung around like a rag doll, but kept his hold on the jaws.

I whipped my head to Tillit. "Can you hit it with Xander there?"

He pursed his lips and shook his head. "No chance, and even if I could they'd be burned to nothing again."

My eyebrows crashed down as I swept my eyes over the area. It was then I saw we stood in the old square. There was the vine curtain through which Thatch had led us. In the center of the clearing stood the remains of the fountain.

My eyes widened. The fountain. I rushed forward and grabbed the tall side to lean over the pool. A shallow bit of water, gathered from rain and the humid air, covered the bottom.

I leaned back and looked at my hands. "Come on. I need you," I whispered. Nothing happened. I frowned and shook them. "I need to save him!"

They lit up like a newly revived string of Christmas lights, if the string only had blue bulbs. I stretched out one glowing hand and held the palm toward the water. The surface bubbled and foamed, and from the froth rose two long, lanky water dragons. Their bodies were smooth and shimmering, and no thicker than my arm but more agile than a fish. Their heads were more pointed than the thick dragon skulls, and their eyes were glowing white orbs.

They curled around each other and paused ten feet above me where they looked down with their unblinking bright eyes. I stretched out my hand and they lowered their heads so I could pet their wet surfaces. "I need your help," I whispered.

"Hold on, My Lord!" Tillit shouted.

I spun around to see Xander still with his hold on the jaws, but with his body slipping over the slippery scales of the creature. The mad dragon reached up a claw and tried to pry him loose. He kicked at it with his feet and the dragon was forced to drop his claw to maintain balance.

I rushed toward the dragon and cupped my hands over my mouth. "Get out of the way!" I shouted. Xander glanced over his shoulder at me. I pointed at the dragons. "Get out of the way!"

Xander leapt out of the way. The dragon opened its mouth and deep in its throat I could see the charge of its fire breath. My slippery serpents rose from the fountain and rushed into the mouth of the mutant. Their wet bodies doused the walls and tongue before they dove into the back. The dragon's fire breath blasted from deep inside its throat and hit my little dragons. Steam burst out of its mouth and a few stray fireballs shot off in all directions.

Tillit and I hit the ground, me on my side and he on his stomach. Xander slid beside me and covered me with his body as we were doused with a hot fog. The monster emerged from its own billowing mist and opened its jaws. The creature's aim was off as it missed us by a body length and staggered to its left away from us. Red spots appeared all over its body like harsh rashes. They grew darker and darker until columns of flames burst through its flesh and high into the air.

We climbed to our feet and Tillit glanced at me. "What did you put in those dragons?"

I shook my head and blinked at the sight. "I thought just water."

"I do not believe this is any of your doing," Xander spoke up.

ISLAND OF THE DRAGON

We stepped back away from the hot fire and watched the dragon writhe in agony. It let out a weak cry and tumbled chin-first to the ground. The fire spread across its body and in a minute its body was a mess of charcoal.

My wide eyes turned up to look at Xander's tense face. "That...that could've been you," I whispered.

He nodded without looking away from the remains of the creature. "Yes. I believe that is what Drake intended."

"So much for a great power," Tillit quipped. He turned to me and raised an eyebrow. "Speaking of power, where'd you learn to use water without touching it?"

"From the school of hard knocks," I quipped as I glanced over my shoulder.

"That must have been a long session," he commented.

Xander looked up at the sky with its waning sun and frowned. "We must finish this before the day is out, or we may not have another chance."

Tillit tucked the tube into his satchel and grinned. "I don't think we're going to have a problem with those Red Dragons getting big and flying over the sea to-" He frowned as his eyes fell on Xander. "I know that look, My Lord, and I don't like it."

Xander's gaze remained on the dead beast. "Before Drake ordered us pushed into the pool he stated that I would be the first of many."

I pointed at the large, burning corpse. "Yeah, but if they're going to last that long he's going to need to bring a pool to the continent, and he's going to have to find another one because I pretty much drained that one."

"Or perhaps he has found a way to neutralize the adverse affects and has hidden away some of the stock," Xander countered.

Tillit snapped his fingers. "Philippus! He knows more than a thing or two about healing potions. I'd bet my last drachma he might have figured something out for his insane lord."

Movement caught my attention. I looked up at the sky and my eyes widened before I pointed up at the barracks. "Speaking of minions, we have a problem."

The men followed my movement and glimpsed the dozen overgrown weards that flew from the windows of the stone building. They flew down the hill toward us with swords in their hands and killer intent in their eyes.

Xander opened his mouth and pointed down the hill. "R-"

"Run this way!" Tillit ordered us as he rushed headfirst into the brush. Xander and I glanced at each other. Tillit paused a few feet into the thick jungle and looked over his shoulder with a frown. "Give Tillit a little more credit."

We shrugged and rushed in after him.

ISLAND OF THE DRAGON

CHAPTER 2

I stumbled through the tough jungle gasping for breath in the humid air. "You. . .you know, I don't think the. . .the boat's a good idea right now."

Tillit glanced over his shoulder and shook his head. "The boat's not an option anymore, but Tillit has another for you."

We rushed down the hill with our sus friend in the lead. He meandered through the thick jungle like parts of the jungle floor were lava. I looked over my shoulder and my heart dropped into my stomach. Our foes were a hundred feet behind us and closing as they swooped between the thick trees. Some of them used their swords to slice through branches in their path and the limbs fell away like cut butter. I cringed as I imagined my head as one of those dismembered branches.

"I hope. . .you're taking us some place. . .with a lot of neck armor," I shouted at our guide.

We reached a small, flat clearing, and Tillit slid to a stop and turned around to face our foes. "No need," he told me.

I heard a strange whoosh behind us and stopped to look back again. A large branch had swung free of its tree and, supported by an assortment of thick vines, flew through the air over our trail. It slammed into the sides of four of the twelve, knocking them from the sky and into the brush. There came a snapping of twigs and sharp cries as they disappeared into the ground.

The other eight flew onward toward us, but only made it half the distance before a vine net dropped from the high canopy. Its ends were weighed down with rocks and stakes that pulled another four to the ground. The leafy foliage that covered the jungle floor gave way and they disappeared into another large hole. Another two were dispatched by a net made of vines that popped up from below and folded them into its impenetrable embrace.

That left the final pair. They ducked and dodged duplicate traps of those already sprung and were close enough to our position that they drew their swords back to slash at us.

I stepped back to avoid the sharp blades, but Tillit grabbed my shoulder. "Steady."

The dragons were two feet from us when Tillit lifted one heavy foot and stomped on the ground. A loud report sounded beneath us and from the ground flew dozens of small, wet balls of leaves, rocks, and vines, all held together by a sticky substance. The balls slammed into the final two dragons and knocked them backward. They hit the ground on their backs and the balls broke open, oozing over their bodies and sticking them to the ground, and that ended our present foes.

I pointed at the glue-covered pair. "What was that?"

"You can't believe that Tillit made his paper vampire tube himself?" Tillit returned.

ISLAND OF THE DRAGON

"Admirable work," Xander complimented him.

Tillit folded his arms over his chest and admired his work. "Not bad, if I do say so myself."

I shook my head at all the countless traps and returned my attention to Tillit. "How long were we captured?" I asked him.

"Most of the day which is how long it took me to make all those wonderful traps," Tillit told me. "The two captains sailed off in the boat to try to find one of their ships. They'll come back as soon as they can."

"So how come you guys weren't captured, too?" I wondered.

"Why fish for the minnows when you have the bass?" Tillit pointed out.

"And how come there weren't more weards?" I added.

Xander gazed up at the barracks and pursed his lips. "Why fish for the minnows when you have the bass?"

"Meaning what exactly?" I asked him.

"As we were discussing before the interruption, the new lord of the Red Dragons no doubt has his hands full with preparations to move the contents of the pool to the continent, and there unleash the powerful beasts," Xander explained.

"And Philippus is just the dragon we need to see," Tillit chimed in. He rummaged through his bag and pulled out a pair of false beards. "I've been saving these for a special occasion," he commented as he passed the beards to us.

I turned my beard over in my hands and looked back to Tillit. "But where's yours?"

Tillit patted his stomach. "I wouldn't fit so well into there clothes. Besides-" he gave me a wink, "-I'm going to be the bait."

I blinked at him. "You?"

He frowned. "Can't I be bait?"

"Only if someone's trying to catch a whale," I quipped.

"We have little time for jest," Xander spoke up as he pulled most of the attire off a man, including the sash. He robed himself in the clothes, pasted the beard on his face and turned to Tillit. "What is your plan?"

A snort escaped me before I clapped my hand over my mouth. Tillit covered his mouth with his fist and cleared his throat. "My Lord, let me help you with that."

Xander arched an eyebrow. "With-" I pointed at his upper chest. He looked down and frowned. The beard was crooked so that one side of his chin peeked out.

Tillit gathered himself and stepped up to Xander where he readjusted the disguise. "My plan is for you two to capture me and drag me back to the barracks where I'll convince the brutes in there that Philippus needs to see me."

"Why would he need to see you?" I asked him.

He grinned and patted the side of his bag. "This thing has more than just tubes and beards, and Philippus knows that."

I tucked the beard and mustache onto my face and grabbed a sash from another unconscious dragon. "

"A moment!" Tillit spoke up. He pulled a can out of his bag and popped open the lid. Inside the can was a black ink-like substance. He held it out to us. "Stick your fingers in here and we'll tie these guys up so they won't try to catch up to us."

Attired and blackened, we dropped the hanging weards into the holes and rolled heavy logs over the tops. A few large leafs and a light splattering of dirt, and the holes were indistinguishable from the ground.

Then, our job finished, Tillit stepped in front of us and together Xander and I marched him up the hill. A half hour later we found ourselves at the base of the barracks. The foundation was made of the same white rock as the rest of the ruined city and rose some thirty feet above us without

ISLAND OF THE DRAGON

window. Atop the foundation was an ugly wooden building some four stories tall. That part of the structure was not without some single-pane

A pair of metal doors, to be precise. They stood in the very center at ground level and were guarded by two red-sashed dragons. I swallowed the lump in my throat as we walked up to the stone-faced men.

One of them stepped forward and raised his hand. "Halt."

We stopped, but Xander nodded at our captive. "We have a captive."

The guard frowned. "Where's the others?"

Tillit stood straight and grinned. "Let's just say you could cover them with dirt."

Xander shoved Tillit and returned his attention to the guard. "They were killed in the struggle with Ferus Draco."

Our foe narrowed his eyes and pursed his lips. "Wait a moment." He opened one of the creaky doors and slipped inside. A few minutes later the door opened, and out stepped not only the guard but a burly, six-and-a-half foot tall dragon with his wings folded behind him.

He strode up to us and sneered down at Tillit. "This is it?"

"The others escaped, but left this sus behind, sir," Xander explained.

Tillit smiled and bowed his head. "Tillit at your service, and service is-" The large weard backhanded his cheek. I had to clench my teeth to keep from likewise responding.

"You'll only talk when spoken to, got it?" he snapped.

Tillit shook his head. "I don't think Philippus would appreciate that."

The guard frowned. "What's he got to do with this?"

Tillit patted the side of his bag. "I've some a few special somethings in here that he'd like to get hold of."

"Then it'll be taken to him, but without you," the guard snapped. He looked over his shoulder and nodded at one of the others. The man stepped forward and reached out for the strap.

Tillit grabbed the strap with both hands and shook his head. "I wouldn't do that if I were you. This satchel is very particular about who and how it's opened."

The Red Dragon hesitated and looked at his commander. "Then tell us how it's done," the leader demanded.

Tillit clicked his tongue. "That won't solve the 'who' problem. Better just to let me see him. We've got a lot to catch up on, anyway."

The guard narrowed his eyes. "He's lying. Take the bag and see what's in it."

The subordinate nodded. "Yes, captain."

The guard tore the satchel from Tillit, tearing the strap in the process, and set it down on the ground. He knelt in front of it and grabbed the flap. Tillit gently pushed us back as the guard flipped open the bag.

A bone-chilling tempest burst from the bag and flew into the guard's face. He screamed and fell back, his hands clawing at his cheeks. The wind transformed into a tunnel that pulled the dragon into itself. Some of his companions leapt forward, but their leader spread out his arms and stopped them. The wind captured the screaming dragon and drew itself back into the bag, shrinking him inside with it. The flap shut after them and all was quiet.

The leader's mouth was agape, but he gathered himself and whipped his head to Tillit. "What by all the gods was that?" he snapped.

ISLAND OF THE DRAGON

Tillit picked up the bag and smiled at the guard. "That would be a part of the Boreas, the north wind. I managed to bottle some of him up on a trip to the north and put him as a guard dog."

One of the weards glanced at his leader. "Captain?"

The captain's face turned a nice shade of red that matched his sash, but he stepped aside and jerked his head toward the entrance. "Take them to the High Priest."

Xander shoved Tillit forward and we followed our 'captive' into the barracks.

CHAPTER 21

The scent of sweat was nearly overpowering and the humidity was enough to make me burst into sweat. The interior walls of the above-ground part of the barracks were made of some sort of brownish concrete that gave the long hallways a sickly color. Thick wooden doors gnarled and half-eaten by bugs spotted the walls. Electric lighting along the ceiling gave light to even the darkest shadows, and a few flickering bulbs finished the eerie atmosphere.

I sidled up to Xander. "High Priest?" I murmured.

"High Priest was always Philippus's highest aspiration," Tillit whispered.

"So how do we find this guy? Is his ego big enough to have a trail to him?" I wondered.

Tillit smiled and tapped the side of his nose. "Tillit will find him."

We meandered through the maze of ugly passages and up two flight of stairs to one of the far corners that faced in the direction of the city. The doors were fewer and farther between. Tillit stopped at one of the rare entrances and wrapped his knuckle against the wood.

"Enter," came the sharp voice of Philippus.

Tillit opened the door and strode inside with us close at his heels. The room was long and wide, and the floor was covered with long, low tables. On the tables were books, bottles, bulbs, and beakers, all scattered around and stuffed together. The windows to our left and opposite the door were boarded up. A single shut door stood in the far right wall.

Bent over one of the tables was the wizened figure of Philippus. He lifted his eyes from the boiling contents of a beaker and his gaze zeroed in on Tillit. The old dragon sneered at the sus before his eyes flickered to us. "Why have thee brought that filth here?"

Tillit stepped forward and swept himself into a low bow. "And a pleasure to see you, too, my dear Philippus. I have a few questions for you."

Philippus returned his attention to his work. "Escort thy captive from my sight, weards." Xander shut the door behind us. Philippus spun around and glared at him. "Did thee not hear me? Get this swine from my sight!"

Xander pulled off the beard and tossed aside the stinking clothes. "I, too, have questions for you, priest."

Philippus's eyes widened. He opened his mouth, but Tillit opened his satchel and stuck his hand inside. "A squeak out of you and I'll set loose Boreas. He's an even worse housekeeper than you are."

Philippus narrowed his eyes. "Thee would not dare."

"Wouldn't I?" Tillit grabbed either side of his bag and opened the mouth wider. A cold wind flew out and swept away the papers.

"Stop!" Philippus shrieked as he leapt at the flying papers. "Stop this!"

Tillit shut the satchel and stepped to one side as he half-turned to Xander. "He's all yours, My Lord."

Xander stepped up to the shriveled old man and glared down at him. "What do you know of the Sæ?"

Philippus knelt down and plucked a few papers from the floor. "I know what thee knows, that it's gift is beyond compare."

"You mean curse," I quipped.

Philippus stood with his arm full of papers and the wrinkled corners of his lips curled up in a grin. "That is no longer true. I have the cure to its side-effects."

"So that's the wonderfully horrible concoction you've made for your insane lord," Tillit quipped.

"Where is this cure?" Xander questioned him.

Philippus gestured to the area around us. "It is all around thee. My work, my papers, my mixtures and potions."

"But where is the finished product?" my dragon lord persisted.

The old man chuckled. "My lord has taken the vials, and with them he shall become as a god."

"And you will become no longer useful," Xander pointed out.

Philippus sneered. "Those fools haven't enough wit among them to create a single thought, much less duplicate my countless years of study."

Our conversation was interrupted when the earth shook beneath us. Bits of plaster fell off the walls and rained down on us from the ceiling. Philippus stumbled into one of his tables and grabbed hold of the top as he glared at the ceiling. "Have those fools no thought to my experiments!"

There came another violent shake. The lights flickered, eerily illuminating a guard who appeared in the doorway. "High Priest, I have been ordered to evacuate you!"

"What blubbering is this? Why need I leave?" Philippus snapped.

The guard shook his head. "We are under attack. There is no time to-" The world around us rocked violently and I heard a heavy clang of metal behind the door.

Philippus's eyes widened. "My searu!"

The crazy old man turned and rushed to the door which he flung open and through which he disappeared.

"High Priest!" the guard yelled.

Xander came up beside him and knocked him on the side of the head. The weard crumpled to the floor, and my dragon lord looked up at Tillit and me. "I could not allow him to attract further attention."

Tillit glanced at the door through which Philippus had left. "My attention's on where that wrinkled old wizard has got to."

He hurried across the room and through the door with Xander and me close at his heels. We raced into the next room and found ourselves in a small area ten feet by ten feet. The windows to our left were also boarded up to hide the row of eight generators that lined the exterior wall. Their normal humming was punctuated by hiccups and coughs.

Philippus rushed from one to the other playing with the plugs and the controls. "Confound those fools! They shall ruin everything!"

There came another boom and another violently shaking. The generator closest to us tipped over onto its neighbor, creating a wide crack in the side.

Tillit wrinkled his nose. "What's that smell?"

I sniffed the air. A pungent odor hit my nostrils. My eyes widened. "Gas!"

My companions blinked at me. "What is it?" Xander asked me.

Chunks of ceiling fell onto the floor, and with it came the string of lights. They swung precipitously over the growing puddle of gasoline on the floor. A single spark and I'd have the biggest headache of my life.

I grabbed their arms and pulled them backward toward the door. "If we don't get out of here quick we're going to be splattered against the walls!"

Tillit dug in his heels and stretched out toward the frantic old man. "Philippus! Get out of here!"

Philippus didn't raise his head as he struggled to lift the fallen generator off its brethren. His cloak was soaked in the fluid as his face turned red from the effort.

"We have to leave!" I insisted.

Tillit pursed his lips and turned away from his old acquaintance. We rushed from the room and paused in the doorway to look out into the dreary, rubbled-littered hall. Men were running back and forth, some with shovels and others empty-handed. A chorus of screams and shouts echoed up and down the passage accompanied by the cymbals of the crashing building.

A sash-clad dragon appeared down the left-hand hall. It was Drake. His gaze fell on us and the Red Dragon lord's eyes glowed so bright they illuminated the area around him. He strode down the hall in our direction.

Xander pulled us away from the doorway and over to one of the boarded up windows. He picked up one of the tables and threw it through the wood, breaking open a large hole.

There was another crash followed by another earthquake. A flash of light came from the generator room and flames blew out of the door. Xander tossed Tillit over his shoulder and swept me into his arms.

Drake appeared in the doorway and grasped either side of the frame. His blazing eyes fell on us and he ground his lengthening teeth together.

Xander leapt out the window just as an explosion rocked the whole building. His wings burst from his back and stretched out far beyond what I remembered. They also had thicker muscles that drew us quickly away from the barracks.

ISLAND OF THE DRAGON

I glanced over his shoulder and watched a ball of flames blast out the window. The heat scorched my face and the flames licked the tips of Xander's wings. More fireballs blasted the boards from the other windows and sent sharp spikes in our direction.

Xander turned a sharp left and dove low so that his arms brushed the treetops. Tillit's face was as white as a sheet as he clung to my dragon lord's neck. "Remind me never to carry this 'gas' with me."

Xander flew us to the hill that overlooked the city and landed. He set me down and I turned to face the barracks, or what remained of it. The stern structure now resembled a small pox victim with holes that gouged most of the exterior, and a huge corner was missing where the generators had exploded. Red-sashes dragons armed with large buckets flew over the barracks and tried to douse the flames with water. Every splash sent unburned gasoline to another part of the corner, stoking the flames even more.

I glanced at my companions who also studied the remains of the building. "You think he made it?"

Xander pursed his lips. "He is of the tenth generation of dragon lords. It would be unwise to assume that even such a strong blast destroyed him."

I arched an eyebrow. "So what exactly is this tenth-generation power, anyway?"

"The power of our ancestors," he told me.

"I got that, but what could they do?" I persisted.

"Their skin was nearly impenetrable, and their strength was unmatched," he explained. "They could fly through the air as quickly as the fastest bird and-" A whistling noise above our heads made us look up.

A round dark object flew over and hit the ground thirty feet from us. The object threw up rocks and dirt. We flung up our arms to protect our faces from the sharp, hard debris.

Tillit lowered his arms and glanced over his shoulder toward the city. "I think the history lesson needs to wait. We've got more explosive problems than a lack of education."

We turned away from the barracks and hurried to the top of the hill. My companions and I paused at the top of the hill and looked down over the city. The squares and broad streets were pocketed with round craters, but most of the buildings were still intact. An evacuation was occurring at our far left as the residents made their way into the dense jungle on the far side of the island.

The source of all that trouble came from the harbor. At the mouth, floating proudly on the seas with their bows pointed at one another and their sides facing the city, were two massive sailing ships. Each vessel had twenty cannons pointed at the city and they were firing off as quickly as they could be loaded. One of the ships sported the flag of Alexandria. The other had a pair of wing bones crossed over one another with a long dragon skull above them.

Tillit slapped his knee and let out a great, belly-rolling laugh. "I never thought I'd see this sight! The Blå Engel and the Rache together at last!"

"Duck!" Xander shouted as he pulled us to the ground.

One of the cannonballs whistled over our heads and slammed into the base of the barracks, sending dirt debris raining down on us. Tillit raised his head and shook his fist at the ships. "Damn fools and their stupid aim!"

Xander helped me to my feet and pursed his lips. "We must reach the ship as quickly as possible."

"Can you carry us both?" I asked him.

"We have little choice."

Tillit stepped back and held up his hands. "As much confidence as I have in you, My Lord, Tillit doesn't think that's a good-" Another cannonball hurtled past us and slammed into a group of trees. One of them crashed to the ground, missing Tillit by a foot. He stared wide-eyed at the trunk before he returned his attention back to us. "Tillit is ready to try whenever Your Lordship is."

Xander knelt down. "Climb on my back. I will carry Miriam."

Tillit did as he was told and Xander winced as the hefty sus climbed aboard. My dragon lord stood and adjusted Tillit's weight before he swept me into his arms and tightly against his chest. He looked over his shoulder at his rear rider and smiled. "Do not fall off."

"I don't plan on it," Tillit quipped.

CHAPTER 22

Xander leapt into the air and flew over the smoking city to the Blå Engel. The crew were hard at work manning the cannons on the deck and the row beneath it. Several of the seamen leapt at us with sabers drawn and surrounded our little group.

"Belay that, men, and get back to yer cannons!" yelled Captain Magnus as he walked down the stairs from the wheel. His ever-present companion Alice was still attached to his wrist, and she to his. Behind them came Nimeni who kept his distance from his angry captain.

"Where in the devil have ya been?" Magnus snapped at us.

"Trying to avoid death by being eaten, explosions and cannonballs," I quipped.

"Why are you attacking the city?" Xander asked his captain.

"And us," I added.

ISLAND OF THE DRAGON

"We couldn't wait any longer for ya to appear, so we decided to try to get those blasted red-sashed fiends to come out and maybe get a chance at us getting in," Magnus explained.

"Did you ever think maybe you might have buried us underneath one of your cannonballs?" Tillit spoke up.

"Not my gunners," Alice argued.

Magnus glared at her. "Nor mine. They could shoot a bird out of the skies."

"Mine can singe their tail feathers without hurting a bone," Alice boasted.

"Mine can swipe a shot across their beak while they're diving for bugs," Magnus returned.

Tillit stepped between them and held up his hands. "Ladies, you're both beautiful, but can we focus on what's more important right now, and that's staying alive."

Alice turned her nose up and sneered at him. "I'm not afraid to die, and we won't be doing that with my cannons firing."

Xander strode over to the railing and set his hands on the top as he looked out over the city. "Unfortunately, your plan to draw out the Red Dragons may change your advantage."

I joined him at the railing and felt the color drain from my face as I gazed at the city. A cloud of Red Dragons flew up from the smoking ruins of the barracks and descended over the city in our direction. One of them flew high above the others, and the red glow around his body showed him to be Drake. His soldiers lined up in a long row of a hundred and five rows deep. Six of them hovered around Drake with three on each side of him.

I glanced over my shoulder at the captains. "How many seamen do you guys have?"

Alice's eyes were wide as she shook her head. "Not that many."

Tillit stroked his chin. "If that fool Drake gives us enough time I might have something to give to your sailors-"

"Seamen," Magnus and Alice corrected him.

"Seamen then," Tillit corrected himself as his eyes flickered to the line of Red Dragons. "They'll be corpses if we wait too long, and I need a few things."

"What do you need?" Alice asked him.

Tillit furrowed his brow and his piggish nose wrinkled. "A few spices from Ui Breasail, and some silphium."

She frowned. "Silphium isn't easy cheap."

"It will be worth less than nothing if we are dead," Xander pointed out.

"What's yer plan?" Magnus questioned him.

Tillit puffed out his chest and grinned. "I'm going to make some Dragon's Bane."

"You know the secret ingredients?" Xander asked him.

Tillit tapped the side of his nose. "Of course."

My eyes widened. "That's how you knew what it smelled like!"

He swept low into a bow. "No sus has a nose as great as mine."

"Let us hope no sus has faster fingers because our foes will not wait," Xander spoke up.

We all returned our attention to the Red Dragons. The first long row flew down toward us. The others followed in tight formation. Two hundred feet from our position the rows split into two columns, and each column took one of the ships.

Magnus whipped his head to the cannons. "Forget the cannons! Pull out yer swords and prepare for a fight, men!"

The seamen abandoned their posts at the cannons and drew out their sabers just as the Red Dragons reached the deck. The dozens of seamen from below deck raced up the steps and unsheathed their weapons. The dragons slammed into our first row of defenders and thus began an epic clashing of claws and steel. More foes crashed onto the deck and surrounded us.

Xander swung his fist out and punched one overboard before he looked at Tillit. "How quickly can you create the Dragon's Bane?"

Tillit ducked a blow from a dragon and kicked him in the groin. The Red Dragon's eyes bulged out of his head and he clutched his broken family jewels. The sus grabbed him, spun him in a staggering circle and swung him over the side of the ship. "Give me a cabin and the ingredients, and I can have a batch ready in no time at all."

"I don't know if my men can hold them off for that long!" Magnus shouted as he parried a blow and sliced another foe.

"Man up, ya soil brat!" Alice snapped. She took a step back and her foot fell through one of the deck boards. Alice fell to one knee before her foe and jabbed him in the gut. The Red Dragon dropped dead onto the deck. She yanked her foot out of the hole and spun around to glare at Magnus. "I'm not going any farther on this floating driftwood!" She grabbed the chain and gave a yank. "We're going to *my* ship!"

"Not on yer life!" Magnus growled as he skewered a foe.

"That might be what it is, and besides, the silphium is on *my* ship!" she reminded him.

Magnus frowned and sliced the head off a foe. "Fine, ya wench, but not a moment longer on that tub!"

The pair shoved a half dozen Red Dragons out of their way and made a clearing on the deck. Magnus slipped his arms under those of Tillit, and together Alice and he took to the air.

Unfortunately, they had company. The Red Dragons didn't appreciate the rough play of the captains and took to the skies after them.

Xander dispatched another foe and glanced over his shoulder at me. "Miriam, you must protect them!"

My eyes widened. "Me?"

He fended off another dragon and turned to me with a smile. "I have faith in you."

I pursed my lips, but spun around and rushed to the bow of the ship. The Rache floated two hundred feet off the bow. My three friends were halfway to their destination, but with their inconvenient attachment and Tillit's weight the Red Dragons were closing in. I climbed onto the top of the wooden figurehead, a half-naked mermaid with ample assets and a sly smile, and raised my hands toward the water.

"Please work. . ." I whispered.

My palms glowed with the familiar blue light. A wide circle of bubbling water gurgled between the two ships. Two of my favorite dragons burst through the surface and stretched into the sky. They opened their wide, narrow jaws and snatched a half dozen Red Dragons from the air. My pets shook their heads and throttled the dragons before they dropped their chew toys into the water to snatch at more of the foes.

I gasped as something violently rocked the ship from side-to-side. I locked my legs and kept my hands in front of me as I glanced over my shoulder. My eyes widened as I glimpsed Drake standing five feet behind me.

The Red Dragon lord's narrowed, glowing eyes glared at my hands. "So that is how you defeated Ferus Draco. The Sæ granted you the strength of your fae lineage, but I will grant you only a swift death." He strode toward me with his hands at his sides. They stretched into long claws that ended in dagger-sharp points.

I looked back at the Rache. My friends had landed and the captains were now in a full fight with the crew against our foes. Tillit was gone, making the Dragon's Bane behind the closed cabin doors. I dropped my hands and faced our greatest enemy as his shadow fell across me. Drake raised his hand to strike me.

Xander flew across the deck and slammed into Drake's side. The Red Dragon stumbled halfway across the wide deck before he caught himself and faced us. A sly smile slipped onto his lips. "You wish to challenge the might of the ancients? I will have you bow to me before I take your life, Ferus Draco."

Xander grasped the hilt of his sword with both hands and moved one foot forward in a battle position. "My name is Xander Alexandros the Sixth, and I bow to no one."

Drake spread open his arms as his clothes burst apart with his scaly transformation. "Then you will fall at my feet."

CHAPTER 23

Xander leapt at him with Bucephalus glowing brightly. He sliced at the Red Dragon, but the lord ducked and jumped back with a laugh as his girth increased. My dragon lord jabbed and swung, but our foe dodged all the blows.

Drake's voice was now a deep rumble as his face stretched out into a sharp jaw. "Your movements are too slow, Lord of Alexandria, but I will have mercy on you and only use a quarter of my true power."

Xander clenched his teeth and continued with his fruitless barrage of missed blows. One wide swing at Drake's gut gave our foe the chance to grab the blade of the sword between two clawed fingers. He had a growth spurt that increased his height beyond the first cross posts of the masts. The fight between seamen and Red Dragons continued, but they scattered to make room for the expanding Drake. With his new height he lifted Xander off his feet so they were face-to-ugly-face.

ISLAND OF THE DRAGON

Drake was now more dragon than man with scales over his body and a long tail out his back. He grinned a toothy grin full of sharp teeth as he swung Xander back and forth. "A strong grip, Ferus, but I am stronger."

Drake slammed Xander chest-first against the deck. Xander gasped and his grip on his sword was broken. Drake drew the sword up and studied the blade. "A fine weapon, but useless." He tossed it over his shoulder over the deck railing and the blade disappeared into the water.

Xander climbed to his feet and narrowed his eyes. Drake chuckled. "Are you angry with me, Ferus? Perhaps with that strength you may actually touch me."

I could see something wrong in Xander's eyes. They glowed bright red like those of Drake. "Xander!" I shouted, but it was too late.

Xander pushed off from the deck and slammed his body into that of the burgeoning Drake. Drake caught him around the middle and lifted him off his feet. He slammed Xander head-first into the deck, breaking the boards and jabbing one of the cracked pieces of wood into Xander's shoulder. Drake drew him out to his face-height and the large piece of wood came with him, lodged in his body.

Drake twanged the board. Xander clenched his teeth, but didn't cry out. Our foe leaned close to Xander and grinned. "I wonder how much pain you can handle until you scream."

I balled my hands into fists. They glowed a bright blue that enveloped my body. I marched up to the dragon and glared up at him. "Put him down!"

Drake looked past Xander and sneered down at me. "What can a pathetic fae do against a god of dragons?"

I pointed behind him. "That."

He twisted his long neck around to look behind him. One of my blue dragons wrapped around that slim neck and gave a nice, hard squeeze. Drake wheezed and his grip on Xander loosened. My other dragon slipped around over the railing and snatched Xander from his grasp. It set Xander behind me on his back and I rushed to my dragon lord's side. His eyes were shut and his teeth were clenched.

I gingerly touched the wood in his shoulder and he hissed. I looked up at my water dragon over my shoulder. "Can you take it out?"

The dragon slipped around the wood and yanked. Xander grasped the deck as the wood drew out of his body. Blood poured from the wound, but I tore a piece off my ruined disguise and wrapped it around his wound.

He opened his eyes and looked at me. Deep down they still held a distinctly murderous look. He tried to sit up, but I pushed him back down. "You're not going anywhere until we talk," I insisted.

He glared at me. "I do not need-"

I slapped him clean on the cheek. Xander's eyes widened and the murderous look disappeared. I crossed my arms over my chest and glared down at him. "Listen, Xander, you're not going to defeat him by going in there without a brain. We have to think of something-" A deep noise behind me made both of us look over my shoulder. I was in time to see Drake, mouth opened, launch a huge fireball at my dragon. The flame pushed my dragon over the boat and disintegrated it over the water. Drake turned his attention to us and black smoke came out of his nostrils. "-very quickly," I finished.

Drake got down on all scaly fours and strode over to us with each foot shaking the deck of the ship. He crushed friend and foe alike beneath his clawed feet and opened his mouth wide. I could see the buildup of fire deep within his throat.

Xander sat up and grabbed my arm to draw me behind him. My water dragon slipped on front of both of us and glared at Drake. I could feel the scorching heat from ten feet away. Our foe took in a deep breath to launch his weapon.

ISLAND OF THE DRAGON

A glop of goo hit him in the side of the face. Drake stumbled to one side and whipped his head in that direction. Tillit hovered over the bow of the ship between Magnus and Alice. Behind them flew the seamen from Alice's ship, or rather, sea*women*, for her crew was made entirely of females.

In Tillit's hands was his tube gun and on his lips was a wide grin. "I hope you're hungry, Your Lordship, because I have plenty of food for you," he teased.

Drake growled and lunged at them. Tillit opened fire. The tube gun fired shot after shot of the gooey substance. It splattered Drake and most of the deck.

"Out of the way, lads!" Magnus yelled.

The seamen ducked below deck and closed the hatch after them, shutting out the remains of the Red Dragon troops. They were covered by the Dragon's Bane and dropped unconscious as their wings slipped into their backs.

Drake, however, remained not only standing but in his dragon form. A laugh rumbled through his throat as he shook off the Dragon's Bane. "You believe that pathetic mix of herbs can defeat a dragon with the power of the ancients?"

Magnus and Alice dropped Tillit at the bow and landed on either side of him as the sus shrugged. "It was worth a try."

Drake stepped backward toward the railing. "You underestimate my power, and for that I shall show you my true strength."

His girth broke through the railing and he slipped over the side of the vessel out of sight. An explosion of red light burst upward from where he had fallen, and the next moment a huge dragon, larger than even Xander under the influence of the waters of Sæ.

The red eyes of the giant Drake zoomed in on us. He opened his wide jaws and let loose a roar that made the sails flutter. Xander narrowed his eyes and climbed to his feet. He took a step forward, but I grabbed his sleeve.

"What the hell are you doing?" I whispered.

He glanced over his shoulder and smiled at me. "Protecting you with my life."

My eyes widened and I shook my head. "Like hell you-" He broke from my grasp and rushed forward.

His clothes tore apart as with each step he became a dragon. He leapt over the side and-fully transformed-crashed into Drake. Unfortunately, even in his full dragon form Xander was still only half as large as Drake.

Our foe was pushed back by Xander's velocity, but he flung up his rear legs and kicked my dragon lord away. Xander tumbled backwards into the center mast of the ship, breaking it in two before he dropped to the deck.

"My ship!" Magnus shrieked.

Alice grabbed his shoulders and pulled him out of the way as the upper half came crashing down. "Don't be gawking when there's fighting to be had!" she barked at him.

A grin slid onto Magnus's lips. "Yer right, lass. Now's the time to have some fun." His gaze fell on the closed hatch. "Avast, men! Get yer tanned hides out here and protect the ship!"

The hatch flew open and his men charged out with swords over their heads. Nimeni was in the lead. They all stopped when they noticed our gigantic foe off the port side.

"Stop yer gaping and get over to the air!" Magnus snapped.

"Aye, aye, captain!" came the call as they unfurled their wings.

Alice looked up at her crew who now hovered over the starboard side. She raised her sword in the air and pointed at Drake "Attack!"

CHAPTER 24

The scene took on the form of chaos as the crews of both ships attacked Drake at the same time. Some of them only brandished their wings and swords, but others changed their hands into claws. Only Xander was capable of holding his dragon form for any length of time as he shook off his crash and flew into the air. Tillit fired off shot-after-shot, and while he couldn't disable the dragon he could blind our foe with the goop.

Nimeni, a thin sword scabbard across his back, raced across the deck and leapt off the port side. He landed cleanly on Drake's back and drew an impossibly long sword from the scabbard. With both hands he drove the long blade into the dragon's back. His stabs were so fast I couldn't count them all.

I also didn't have time. I wasn't going to be left out of the fun, so I rushed to the port side and pointed my palms at the water. They glowed their beautiful blue color and from the depths of the bay rose my pair of familiars. They stretched upward from beneath Drake and wrapped their lithe bodies around his rear legs, throwing off his balance and granting our side some advantage as the crews attacked.

They needed all the help they could get. Even with his girth Drake was faster and more nimble than the swiftest dragon. He twisted out of the way of many of their blows and brought them down with well-aimed swipes. Many dropped into the water, and some didn't rise back up, at least not on their own.

I commanded one of my dragons to rescue the many crew members who floundered in the water. The other released Drake and began an assault by attacking his sides and underbelly.

Alice and Magnus were among their men fighting the behemoth. Drake swiped at the joined pair. His claws brushed against Alice's side and knocked her out of the air. Magnus was pulled down with her, but he corrected his trajectory and swooped down to catch her in his arms. He glided onto the deck and set her down on the planks.

His soft eyes searched her pale face with her shut eyes. "Alice! Lass! Speak to me!"

Her eyes flew open and she smiled up at him. "Don't count me out of the fight, captain."

A shadow fell over them, and they both looked up in time to watch Xander land with a heavy crash onto the deck. He stood on all fours and his long, scaly tail whipped out. He leapt into the air and his appendage swiped downward. The pair raised their joined arms in instinct to protect themselves and the tail shattered the metal chain into a thousand bits. Alice raised her freed hand and gawked at the ruined chain, but Magnus grabbed her arms and yanked her to her feet.

"Don't be gawking when there's fighting to be had!" he barked at her. She pursed her lips, but nodded and together they leapt into the air.

ISLAND OF THE DRAGON

I felt myself growing a little weak as my water dragon struggled to made any dent in his impenetrable scales. Xander flew backward and opened his mouth. From the depths of his throat he launched a blazing fireball that made the crews scatter.

For a moment our attacks, his fireball and my dragon's bite, collided against Drake's left side. The huge dragon reared back its head and let out a cry of pain as a slithering column of smoke rose from the impact area. Drake flew back away from our attackers and roared at us.

I took a step closer to get a better look at the smoke when my foot slipped on the deck. I looked down and found myself staring at the green-and-blue flag of Alexandria. The countless airborne dragon men and women made it flutter and ripple like the wings of a dragon and the water of the oceans.

My eyes widened. I whipped my head up and found Xander hovering near the bow of the ship. I rushed to the bow and hurried up to stand beside Tillit who grinned at me. "You two seem to have broken the myth about an impenetrable dragon."

I looked straight at Xander and cupped my hands together over my mouth. "Xander! Shoot the biggest fireball you can at him!"

"An Adisesha should do it," Tillit added.

Alice whipped her head in our direction and glared at us. "Even a lord of dragons can only do that once, and if it doesn't work we're fish bait to this monster."

Xander flew close to the bow and gazed into my eyes. I smiled back at him. "We can do this together, partner."

A smile slipped onto his wide, long-snouted lips and he nodded. Xander flew away and closer to Drake. The crew members flew out of the line of battle, leaving an empty corridor between the pair. Our foe narrowed his eyes and opened his mouth wide. Xander did the same, and the combined heat from their throats made the water between them boil.

    I stepped up to the very edge of the port side and raised my hands. My water dragons rose from the water and stood before me. They stretched their long necks toward me so their noses were only a foot from me. Their soft glowing eyes stared into mine.

    I reached out my hands and stroked their wet noses. "We need your help," I whispered to them. I leaned my forehead against first one and then the other. "*I* need your help."

    The dragons nuzzled my cheeks before they drew back and turned to face the dueling dragons. I grinned and raised my glowing hands. "All right, let's do this."

    The flames in the throats of the dragons grew brighter. Drake and Xander drew their heads back for the shot and launched their fireballs. Drakes ball was three stories tall and just as wide. Xander's was half the height, but the pair of them both left behind them sparking orange tails like those of meteors.

    My dragons rushed forward faster than the swiftest bird and wrapped themselves around Xander's fireball. Rather than extinguish the ball of fire the bright orange color changed to green. The blue light of my dragons burst outward like a supernova and together the colors lit up the whole of the bay with their light.

    The fireballs collided in an explosion of heat and color. They pushed against one another in a furious battle that sent sparks flying and stirred the waters beneath them into a whirlpool.

    Xander's ball began to lose the battle. Drake's fireball slowly swallowed the beautiful green-blue light until it was completely gone.

    Our foe laughed. "Pathetic. Even together you are-" He paused and frowned.

Rather than continuing on its trajectory Drake's fireball hovered in place. The sparks on its tail flickered and lost their luster. Then, from the rear, came the familiar green-blue light of Xander and my flame. Our fireball burst through the back of Drake's ball, and without our flame his toy imploded.

Drake's eyes widened as our fireball careened toward him. He tried to twist out of the way, but the blue light slipped in his direction like a lithe dragon and struck him straight in the chest. He let out a terrible roar as the brilliant light engulfed him. His wings and scales fell away as his body shrank back to his human form. His shining red eyes glared at Xander and me one final time before they closed and he fell backward out of the flaming ball.

His body crashed into the water and sank below the surface. Our fireball disappeared, and all was quiet. It was done. We had won.

CHAPTER 25

A whoop came out of Tillit. "You two did it!"
A cry of joy arose from the crews. They flew
Xander turned, but his wings faltered. He fell from the sky as his body transformed back into his human form. Magnus leapt over his ship and caught our dragon lord before he hit the water. The captain brought him back aboard and lay him on the deck.

We crowded around him and I cupped his cheek. His eyes fluttered open and he smiled up at me. "Good job, partner," I whispered.

He grasped my hand and returned my smile with one of his own. "It could not have been done without both of us."

Tillit cleared his throat. "Does Tillit not deserve some credit?"

ISLAND OF THE DRAGON

I laughed. "And Tillit-" Magnus and Alice stepped up behind him. Behind *them* stood their crews. "-and everyone else," I added.

Tillit pulled out some large bottles of drink and grinned. "Then why not a little celebration to congratulate ourselves?"

"Belay that for a moment," Magnus spoke up as he swept his arm over the ruined deck of his ship. There were fallen Red Dragons who would never again open their eyes, but many more who were merely unconscious from the effects of the Dragon's Bane. "

"The punishment for breaking their exile is death," Alice spoke up.

"That's a sentence only a lord can make," Tillit pointed out.

All eyes fell on Xander. He studied the prone Red Dragons and pursed his lips. "While their intentions were to leave the island they went no further than their fishing allowed. The dragon who did break the rule has been punished. For the others we will fly them to the beach and leave them there for their families to find." His eyes flickered to the pair of captains. "Will your crew handle the arrangements?"

Captain Magnus grinned and nodded. "Aye, and be glad to be done with them."

Alice glared at him. "Yer too soft. If it was up to me I'd be throwing them overboard."

Magnus wrapped his arm around her waist and grinned down at her. "If I'm getting soft then I need a good woman to make me hard, if ya know what I mean."

Alice rolled her eyes and pressed one palm against his chest to push away. "Only too well."

He tightened his grip on her. "If ya think I'm letting ya go again yer more daft than I am, lass. Why don't we get married?"

She narrowed her eyes. "On who's ship?"

"Mine, of course."

"Then the wedding's off because if we're going to be on a ship it's going to be mine."

"Why don't you guys just get married *between* your ships?" I suggested.

Magnus arched an eyebrow. "In a boat?"

"Use those dragon wings and be in the air," I explained.

Magnus grinned down at his bride. "What do ya think, lass? Up for another try?"

A coy smile slipped onto her lips. "I would, but we'll be needing a preacher."

Tillit stepped forward and puffed out his chest. "It just so happens that I'm an ordained priest in the church of Alexandria."

My jaw dropped open. "*You?*"

He glanced at me and frowned. "Why does everyone doubt Tillit's talents?"

Xander patted him on the shoulder. "Perhaps if you gave us a list we would not be so surprised."

Magnus turned to the crews as did Alice by his side. "Ya heard yer lord, men, get to it so we can get to the wedding!"

"Show these men what true seamen can do, and someone help me on with that blasted dress!" Alice called to her women.

The crews got to work clearing the decks of both ships while the main mast of Magnus's ship was repaired. I sidled up to Xander and touched his arm. He turned to me and I smiled up at him. "Your mom would be proud of you."

He returned my smile with one of his own. "I believe you are right."

In an hour both jobs were done and the sun was beginning to set as the ships sailed away from the inhospitable harbor and out into the open seas. We stopped just out of sight of the island with the ships fifty yards apart.

ISLAND OF THE DRAGON

All the crew members not injured flew out and filled the gap while the others, including Nimeni, crowded the decks. Two of the fliers held up Tillit in the middle while Xander held me in his arms. All was quiet as the setting sun provided the backdrop to the ceremony.

The bride arose from her ship dressed in a white wedding dress bedecked with pearls. The train was so long that six of her crew held it up to keep it from dropping the twenty feet into the water. Magnus arose from the deck of his own ship clothed in a suit of dark navy blue. They met at Tillit and turned to face the impromptu preacher.

Tillit smiled at both of them. "We are gathered here to join the sky and the sea in the most ancient of unions."

I looked up at Xander. "'Sky and sea?'" I whispered.

He nodded. "The sea is not so beautiful without the sky."

"If anyone knows why these two should not be joined, speak now or forever keep your mouth shut," Tillit added.

Magnus glared at his crew. They flew at attention except for those who needed to blow their noses. Alice was all blushing-bride and smiles. Some of her crew wiped their faces across their sleeves.

"Then by the blessing of Valtameri I pronounce you joined. You may kiss the-" Alice wrapped her arms around Magnus's neck and kissed him passionately on the lips.

A whoop and a holler arose from both factions as they all joined in on the kissing. A crew member from each ship flew low and dipped a goblet into the seas before they flew to the happy pair. They parted and each took a glass.

Magnus grinned at his bride. "May we have a long life together, lass."

Alice raised her glass to him. "And may you never grow fat," she teased.

A bright light caught the attention of the wedding party, and we all looked up at the sky. A beautiful rainbow stretched across the sky. At its origin was a bird with long, bright plumage.

I furrowed my brow. "Is that a-"

"Phoenix," Xander finished for me.

Magnus raised his glass to the bird and smiled. "Here's one to ya, captain, and a pardon from me."

The festivities began and lasted long after the sun had set. By the light of countless torches the mingled crews danced and drank the night away. At about midnight I was nearing an empty mug when I noticed my dragon lord had vanished. I found him at the railing peering out on the water with an untouched mug by his side.

I joined him at the railing and looked out on the calm, moonlit seas. "You're worried about something," I commented.

He nodded. "Yes. Philippus informed us that Drake was in possession of the altered Sæ, and yet I could see no evidence that it was used."

"That's because he thought he could beat us," I pointed out.

"But then where did the concoction go?" he countered.

My shoulders slumped and my face fell. "Did you have this much trouble *before* you got me?"

He chuckled. "No, and much of it was my own doing."

I arched an eyebrow. "Such as?"

He lifted his chin a little and furrowed his brow. "There was this very beautiful young barmaid in Síol-that is, Cayden's capital-who betrayed us to some kidnappers."

I snorted. "She sounds nice."

ISLAND OF THE DRAGON

"We were both quite young at the time, but apparently the bounty on us was a considerable sum," he added.

"I'm sure she felt bad about doing it and wiped her tears away with gold coins," I quipped.

He chuckled. "I am sure she did, though we never saw her again. Cayden and I managed to escape and our fathers razed our captors' lair to the ground as a warning to others."

I turned my head to him and studied his face. "Speaking of warning, what are you going to tell everyone about dragons and humans?"

Xander pursed his lips and shook his head. "I do not know."

"Why not keep telling them what you've always told them," Tillit spoke up as he emerged from the festivities and joined us at the railing.

Xander arched an eyebrow. "And what is that?"

"That we all need to stop killing each other and live together," he reminded him.

I smiled. "It's an idea so crazy it just might work."

"Speaking of ideas, I've got one," Tillit continued as he took a swig from his mug. He used the mug to point at us. "If you two find yourselves in another adventure could you count me out of it? Just this once?"

Xander chuckled. "You were not counted among our company at Bha na Ruin, but I am sure an adventure is not forthcoming."

I pursed my lips and turned to face the dark waters around us. Xander arched an eyebrow and sidled up beside me. "You find that thought disturbing?"

I set one elbow on the railing to cup my chin in my hand. The gentle seas around us rocked the boat to and fro.

A small smile slid onto my lips as I nodded. "I don't know why, but it's just-I don't know, I guess it's a little sad to be done with all of it." A thought came to my mind that made me snort. "Maybe it's like what another Alexander said in my old world. 'There are no more worlds to conquer.'"

"I'm sure you two will find more adventures," Tillit spoke up as he raised his mug to us. "And here's to your many more victories."

Xander and I raised our mugs in the air and we all smiled. "To victory, and to adventure."

The many more we were destined to have, and far sooner than I expected.

A note from Mac

Thank you for purchasing my book! Your support means a lot to me, and I'm grateful to have the opportunity to entertain you with my stories.

If you'd like to continue reading the series, or wonder what else I might have up my writer's sleeve, feel free to check out my website at *macflynn.com*, or contact me at mac@macflynn.com.

* * *

Want to get an email when the next book is released? Sign up for the Wolf Den, the online newsletter with a bite, at *eepurl.com/tm-vn*!

Continue the adventure

Now that you've finished the book, feel free to check out my website at **macflynn.com** for the rest of the exciting series.

Here's also a little sneak-peek at the next book:

Myths Beyond Dragons:

> They just wouldn't stop popping up. Like those dots you see when you look at the sun too long, no matter how hard I tried to look away the visions were still there.
> That's why I stood at the edge of the lake in Alexandria. The shoreline was touched by ice, but three yards into the lake the water lay open. The shadows didn't touch me here, or so I hoped. Behind me towered the ancient water temple, and between us stood the arch that guided the path up to the religious building.
> I raised my hand and studied the palm. The tips of my fingers were a little red, but the unmistakable color of my skin gave me comfort.
> A cool breeze blew past me and across the late, disturbing the tranquil scene for a brief moment. I wrapped my coat tighter around myself and shivered. "You'd think a water fae wouldn't get cold. . ." I muttered.
> "Temperature and water are very different," a voice spoke up. I spun around and found Xander walking

down the path toward me with a teasing smile on his face.

My own face fell as he came up beside me. "How'd you know I was here?"

He nodded at my covered shoulder. "I always know where you are."

I pressed my hand on the part of my coat that lay over the mark and looked out over the lake. The water was as calm as glass, and just as reflective. The castle across the lake was illuminated with candles, and a perfect picture of it lay on the watery surface.

"Something troubles you," Xander spoke up.

I snorted. "Does my mark tell you that, too?"

He gently cupped my chin in his hand and turned my face so we gazed into each other's eyes. His were penetrating. "I do not need help to know when you are bothered, I need only your help to tell me what it is that bothers you."

I bit my lower lip and cast my eyes to the ground. "I'm not really sure myself, and it's really hard to explain."

"I will try to understand," he replied.

My eyes flickered up to his face and I frowned at him. "This isn't funny. I really think there's something wrong with me."

His eyebrows crashed down and all humor fled his face. "You are ill?"

I shook my head. Then I shrugged. "I don't know." A snort escaped my lips. "With all the weird things that have happened, this has to be the weirdest."

"Have your headaches returned?" he guessed.

I shook my head. "No, but-" I jumped as a flock of snowbirds flew out of a nearby tree and headed out over the lake.

Xander smiled down at me. "There is nothing to fear so long as we are together."

I looked out over the lake and pursed my lips. "I'm not sure we can do this-" There came the sound of a single drop of water hitting the surface of a puddle. The sound was faraway, like an echo from a distant world.

I froze, and so did the rest of the world. The flock of birds that flew over the lake were frozen in mid-flight. The breeze no longer stirred the bare branches of the trees. The colors became muted, as though someone had taken most of the life out of the world. The cold that had chilled me now sank into my bones. My shoulders slumped and I pinched the bridge of my nose. "Not again. . ."

Then I remembered I wasn't alone. A smile stretched across my face as I spun around. Xander stood behind me, but he, too, was a muted statue. My face fell. I walked up to him and reached up my hand to cup his cheek.

"Et tu, Xander?" I whispered as I stroked the smooth, warm surface. Wait, warm?

His eyes fluttered like he had just awoken and he stumbled forward like a man walking out of a moving vehicle that had suddenly stopped. I caught him before he fell onto the ice and stared up at him with wide eyes.

"You're awake?" I whispered.

He shook himself and raised his head to look at the colorless world around us. "What has happened to Alexandria?"

I steadied him and swept an arm over the timeless area. "Welcome to my world, or what's been my world off-and-on for a few months."

"Is this your old world?" he asked me.

I shook my head. "Nope. Mine had just as much color as yours especially when someone painted their house purple."

"How did we come to be here?" He glanced down at me and tilted his head to one side as he studied my face with a furrowed brow. "Is this some new power you have?"

I cringed. "I hope not, and if it is I don't feel myself using my energy. Besides-" I held up one of my hands, "-no glow."

He raised his eyes to the lake and pursed his lips. "Then perhaps were are in another-" he frowned.

I half-turned and followed his gaze. His eyes lay on the lake. The reflective surface showed the castle. Its colors were as they should have been, but the castle across the lake was the drab one.

"That's. . .that's the castle, isn't it?" I guessed.

Xander nodded. "It is. We are in a reflection of our world." He returned his attention to me and grasped both my hands so we faced each other. "Tell me everything you know."

I shrugged. "It's not that much. I hear this drop of water hitting more water and suddenly everything becomes a black-and-white movie."

He arched an eyebrow. "A 'movie?'"

I shook my head. "Never mind. Everything loses its color and everything stands still."

"And you touched no one else?" he wondered.

I snorted. "I touched everything I could think of hoping it would be my red slippers out of this world, but nothing happened until I tried you."

"Then you had not tried me before?" he guessed.

I shrugged. "I'm not usually in here that long, or even this long. Usually it's just long enough for me to panic and start slapping my hand against walls and people, and then I'm snapped back into the Wonderful World of Color."

"How long have you been coming to this world?" he questioned me.

"Two months."

He frowned at me. "And you spoke nothing of this to me?"

I bit my lower lip and lowered my eyes. "I. . .I kind of thought I was going a little nuts, you know? Like maybe I'd been whacked around a little too much by a Red Dragon and was imagining all of it."

Xander lifted his gaze to the mute world around us and pursed his lips. "Unfortunately, it is very much real, and we are both a part of it for the present."

I smiled up at him. "I'm glad you're the one who's with me. Well, not glad you're with me, but-"

He chuckled. "I understand." He took my hand and guided me toward the arch. "Together we will search the library and contact Apuleius to learn what he may know-" We walked beneath the arch and came out in a whole new world.

We stumbled forward as the incline of the short hill straightened to a flat wood floor. I looked up and saw we were surrounded by floor upon balcony-lined floor of bookshelves filled to the top with books. Far above us was a glass dome that allowed bright light to illuminate the countless floors filled with knowledge, along with a walkway that stretched out from our floor into the void in the center of the circular structure to a free-standing platform that looked out over all of the books.

Xander stepped forward with his mouth agape and looked up at the skylight. "Is this the fabled Mallus Library?"

I followed him and frowned. "Yeah, but how'd we get here without a door?"

"Even an archway is a door to a new place," a voice spoke up.

We both turned to the free-standing pathway to see Crates striding down it toward us. He slipped around the corner and stopped a few feet from where we stood with a smile on his face. His gaze fell on Xander and he inclined his head. "It is an honor to meet the son of Cate, wife of Alexander the Tenth."

Xander arched an eyebrow. "You knew my mother?"

Crates nodded. "Yes. She was very curious and often found herself here in search of answers." He chuckled. "At one point her visitations were so often I wondered if I shouldn't make a room for her."

"So were we brought here so you could give us a book only Tillit can read on how to paint the world?" I asked him.

Crates shook his head. "On the contrary. It is I who need you."

Other series by Mac Flynn

Contemporary Romance
Being Me
Billionaire Seeking Bride
The Family Business
Loving Places
PALE Series
Trapped In Temptation

Demon Romance
Ensnare: The Librarian's Lover
Ensnare: The Passenger's Pleasure
Incubus Among Us
Lovers of Legend
Office Duties
Sensual Sweets
Unnatural Lover

Dragon Romance
Blood Dragon
Dragon Bound
Maiden to the Dragon

Ghost Romance
Phantom Touch

Vampire Romance
Blood Thief
Blood Treasure
Vampire Dead-tective
Vampire Soul

Urban Fantasy Romance
Death Touched

Werewolf Romance
Alpha Blood
Alpha Mated
Beast Billionaire
By My Light
Desired By the Wolf
Falling For A Wolf
Garden of the Wolf
Highland Moon
In the Loup
Luna Proxy
Marked By the Wolf
Moon Chosen
The Moon and the Stars
Moon Lovers
Oracle of Spirits
Scent of Scotland: Lord of Moray
Shadow of the Moon
Sweet & Sour
Wolf Lake